Edge of

CW00349600

Fiona Firth

chipmunkapublishing
the mental health publisher

Published by

Chipmunkapublishing
PO Box 6872
Brentwood
Essex
CM13 1ZT
United Kingdom

http://www.chipmunkapublishing.com

Copyright © Fiona Firth 2012

Edited by Aleks Lech

ISBN   978-1-84991-737-7

Chipmunkapublishing gratefully acknowledge the support of Arts Council England.

Fiona Firth

Thank you
to David Firth, Robert Firth and
Bill Ions for all their help.

The Edge Of The City

Author Biography

Fiona Firth was born in Newcastle in 1973. She qualified as a Learning Disability Nurse in 2001 and feels passionately about the rights of disabled individuals, particularly their right to make choices about their own lives. She has experience of learning disability hospitals, resettlement homes, day services and community teams.

She has an additional interest in mental health and recently studied psychological wellbeing at Newcastle University.

Fiona lives in Northumberland with her husband, David and two daughters, Charlotte and Anna. She runs an inclusive childminding service and plays horn in a local band.

The Edge Of The City

Chapter 1

Oakwood - 1955

Jess sat on the wooden bench, the noise of the shower drowning out the shouting. Not that she could hear it; after the first six weeks her body had learned how to shut out the noise around her. It was months now since she had arrived at Oakwood, she wasn't sure how many. At first she tortured herself asking "Why?" Why did her mother leave? Why did her dad bring her here? Why was she left in a waiting room with a duffle bag and a piece of paper?

"I've packed a change of clothes and she has her birth certificate" her dad told a lady in a dark blue uniform. "I would have kept her; I wanted to, but with my wife…" - he paused - "gone, I need to work".

"It's for the best" the lady assured him.

He shuffled across the floor towards where Jess sat, his shoulders hunched and fiddling with his cap. His eyes were red as though he hadn't slept in days, and sweat dripped down his forehead.

"Jess," he took a deep breath and sighed.

"Good bye Jess, I…"

He left sniffing and shaking.

So she sat now, naked and cold. Water trickled round her feet.

"Next!" a voice shouted.

An older lady sat next to her, got up and walked to the shower. They hosed her down and washed her wrinkly body with the same cloth as they had used for the first twelve ladies. They soaped and rinsed her grey tufty hair.

"Next!" Jess knew what to expect

"Arms up".

She obeyed. It was quickly over. She was given a wet towel and picked up some clean clothes.

"First up best dressed" the nurses used to laugh. Jess didn't see why that was funny, although it was true. No one had their own clothes. You helped yourself from the cupboard in the corridor. All the dresses were put into two piles and you took what you wanted. Nothing fitted properly and everything was made on site. Vanity wasn't accommodated at Oakwood.

Outside the ward where she lived was the bank leading up to the big stone building, with big doorways and small narrow windows. The cars were parked outside – just the way her dad's had been on the day she arrived. Around it was a beautiful grassed garden with colourful flower beds and neatly cut grass. Small windy paths linked the wards to the rest of the site. Jess had wondered if this was like most villages. It had a shop, a church, the workshops, a nursery, a post box, a bakery and even a farm. It was not unlike her own village at home.

The new wards were brick buildings with flaking green paint on the external guttering and double doors. Around 55 women lived on Jess' ward. With twenty beds in each of the three rooms, there were always a couple empty.

"Ward 18a" she'd been told. "That's where you're going, it's a high grade ward so there'll be others to talk to."

"High grade?"

"Yes, others like you that can walk and talk – help out more, you'll fit right in."

Whatever it was it had to have been better than the three nights on the admissions ward.

Oakwood was its own world, sheltered from reality by the imposing trees and miles of farm land. It was near enough to the city that the occasional visitors could reach, yet far enough away so as not to offend the civilisation of normality.

There were weekly visits to the local village, where the best behaved would line up two by two like a school trip. In matching grey clothes and short neat haircuts they would parade, without destination, through the town. It was a familiar site in the village; no one took much notice as most of the villagers worked at the hospital anyway. The children were the worst – they'd giggle and shout, and sometimes they threw things if no one reacted to them.

There were no individual outings. No one was allowed off site unless with the written permission of the hospital doctor and even then, it was only for an hour with staff – no one really bothered.

Jess pulled up her skirt; she could smell the porridge from the corridor. It was always the same. Tea with sugar and milk, already in the large pot with porridge and toast. She walked down the bleak corridor, past the large dormitories, her blouse still sticking to her back where she hadn't dried herself properly.

Two nurses stood in the corridor, one holding a large bottle of medicine and a sticky looking teaspoon.

"There's got to be an easier way of making a living than this" one said.

"No, not as entertaining, never two days the same" the other corrected.

Jess didn't know what they meant – all days seemed the same to her.

Get up

Shower

Breakfast and tablets

Workshop

Lunch

Workshop

Tea break

Workshop

Dinner and tablets

Supper

Bed and tablets

Everything worked as clockwork, there was no need to
learn the time or read a calendar, this was all you
needed to know. Except Sundays; Jess liked Sundays
– they went to church and sang, she liked to sing. Even
if she didn't know any of the words it was calming and
comforting.

Jess looked around the dining room. She wasn't like
the others, they weren't normal she thought, they
looked different and made noises as if no one else
could hear them. They'd been here all the time, not like
her, she knew different. She had a mum who loved
her, who read her stories and tucked her up in bed.
Except that was "gone" now. That's what her dad said.

"She's gone, your mum – she can't come back from
there - she would if she could." Her dad looked sad;
she didn't see why, her mum must be coming back
eventually.

From first glance Jess was beautiful. She had long red
hair – till they cut it short - petite features and wide
brown eyes.

"How can she be defective? She's pretty," her dad had
said.

"She'll just take a little longer to learn than the boys,
she's still our little princess," her mum appealed,
putting her arms around Jess's shoulders.

She thought about her brothers, Colin and Derek. They
were older than her by two years. "Born on the same
day" Derek had told her. Identical in looks but not in
nature. Colin was loud and boisterous. He wanted to

make people laugh, not Jess though, he had no interest in Jess. He wasn't mean or horrid like some of the other kids in the street; he just didn't bother with her. She was just in the way, a nuisance. Derek was different, he was quiet and gentle; he had kind eyes the same colour as hers.

"Two peas in a pod," people would say about the twins, "can't tell them apart". Jess could, she might not be able to think well but she knew who her Derek was. After breakfast she returned to her dormitory. The bundle of bedding still lay at the end of the bed. The beds were smaller than proper ones and the gap between them was only just big enough to turn around. There was a mirror on the cupboard at the end of the dormitory. She got out the comb she hid yesterday and looked into the mirror.

She stared into her own eyes; a sudden rush of homesickness hit her as she saw Derek looking back at her. She wanted to see her mum, to play in the back yard, to help set the table and dust the floor. Tears trickled down her cheeks. She was seventeen; was that it now? Was this all there was?

"What are you doing?" a voice shouted

"Stop that nonsense at once! Feeling sorry for yourself will do no good, off to work this minute." She dried her tears and left. That's the last time I let them see me cry, she thought to herself as she set off for the workshop.

Stan Patterson still shook when he returned home from Oakwood. He quickly poured himself a large whisky from his crystal decanter which he never touched, and closed the curtains. He didn't want to be bothered – not today. He didn't want to hear "It's for the best" or "It's where her sort belong".

Closing his eyes, he pictured Betty, his beautiful wife. His heart ached. It was so unfair, she was 39! That's all! If anyone had to die it should be him, goodness knows, he'd come close to it during the war. He was prepared to die; it didn't scare him. Living alone without Betty scared him.

The whisky warmed his chest; he took a deep breath and poured another. What would he tell the boys about Jess? They were away at sea and in the Navy just like he had been a decade earlier. He'd been surprised when they'd both joined up at the end of national service. Probably getting away from the agony of seeing someone you love becoming so helpless and crippled with pain. Two years she'd been ill and no one had prepared him for what to expect. When she eventually did pass away he felt an initial relief, followed by an enormous weight of guilt, then sadness finally finished off by the dreaded feeling of loneliness and despair.

Telling the boys about Jess wasn't something he'd thought about. Colin would be OK, he had nothing to do with Jess, but Derek was different, more like his mother. Colin was loud, always the centre of attention, never short of a girlfriend and very popular at school. Derek was quiet, thoughtful, read a lot and spent most of his time fishing with his best mate Martin.

Sometimes Stan felt it was Derek and Martin that were the twins; they were inseparable.

His hands stopped shaking now. His mouth felt numb as the drink took effect. His thoughts drifted back to Betty. She loved her children; so did he, but not like her. They were her reason for living. Before they got married she worked at a school, not as a teacher, as a typist, but she went out of her way for the children. She'd had the boys shortly after getting married and it had weakened her. The whirlwind energy she once had was calmed, but her enthusiasm, her spirit, her optimism, that never weakened even at the end. Two years after they'd had the twins they had Jess and Stan thought life was complete. She was the most beautiful baby and well behaved too. She didn't seem to cry like the other babies, she was placid and content as if in her own world. Despite that, he never dreamed anything was wrong, he'd never met anyone who was "mentally subnormal." Feeble minded – that's what the doctor had said, as though she could think but couldn't be bothered. Before they knew, he adored her, his only little girl, a little diamond. Had it been her or a creation in his mind to get him through the long nights of the war? He was at sea for most of her early years so he would never know.

All he knew was, it wasn't like he thought – coming home at the end of the war. He dreamt of seeing his little girl (five by now) running towards him and flinging her arms around him. It hadn't been like that at all. He tried and tried for a reaction but she just looked through him.

"Hello sweetheart."

"Urgh!" she said eventually.

"Da da da dah."

"Daddy!" a little voice had shouted; one of the boys, Colin, he thought, but he wasn't sure. The other was only a foot behind. He put his arms out. They'd grown, they were proper little men now.

"Hello boys." He'd pulled them close.

Why was nothing how he planned, or how he thought it would be? He poured himself another glass and gulped it back. It numbed everything, took the edge off reality, but it wouldn't stop the guilt that stayed, hovering in the background continuously.

"You've no need to feel guilty" Mrs Fleeceman had said.

"You've done your best, but it's just not right – a young girl like that being cared for by a man. Oakwood Hall – it's the right thing, the decent thing to do. It's a harsh world out there, you can't spare her from that, they can."

"She's not a child!" he'd protested.

"Yes she is, she always will be – she'll always be a child, never achieve much – not like normal folk anyway." Her voice grew softer now, her eyes were kind.

"And what about you Stan? Don't you deserve a life? Betty's gone but you don't need to be on your own forever, you'll meet someone else and when you do they won't want to take on Jess. It was OK when she was little, but she's a burden Stan, a burden for life. Those people at Oakwood, they understand those sort of people, she'll be with others like herself. She won't get stared at there or made to feel different. She'll be one of them."

There was truth in what she'd said. Mrs Fleeceman had been hired as a housekeeper when Betty was ill – but she'd become a good friend, a confidante, an advisor. She was an older lady, around sixty he thought, and had lots of life experience. Both her sons were killed during the war and her husband was long gone. She was a survivor, she didn't waste time on self pity but dusted herself down and carried on – he'd admired her for that. It wasn't that she was harsh or unfeeling, she was practical and realistic.

"OK" he said quietly after a long silence, "write to Oakwood, see if they'll take her".

"You're making the right choice, one day you'll see that."

He opened his eyes, and the room came back to him – slightly more blurred than before. Everything was quiet – Mrs Fleeceman was out for the day and he hadn't seen the boys since the day after the funeral. Had he done the right thing? He'd never know, not for sure. Would Jess understand? Would she settle? Would she be spared from the harsh realities of life like he'd spared her from the grief of her mother's death?

"She's gone," he'd told her.

"She wouldn't understand and the funeral would just upset her" Mrs Fleeceman had told him.

"Upset everyone if she was there."

She made the arrangements, and he honestly didn't know how he would have coped in those early days without her presence.

"If there's one thing I do know, it's how to arrange a good funeral – the number of people I've had to bury." She had a kind smile; her hair was neat and straight, cut geometrically around her ears. She had a stocky build with thick ankles and big hands. So he'd told Jess her mother had gone, not died, not an angel in heaven, just gone. It was as if he didn't want to say the words out loud. Jess had looked, as she often did, expressionless, glazed and unaffected.

"What's for tea?" she'd said after an uncomfortable silence of Stan thinking she had understood. He wanted to scream "Is that all you can say? Why don't you understand?" but he didn't.

"Mrs Fleeceman will see to it" he said quietly and left the room – Jess still rocking in her chair, humming as when he entered. Maybe she was right, maybe this was for the best. He put the stopper back on the decanter and turned to go to bed. Lying in his room he turned to where his wife once lay. Stroking the pillows, he closed his eyes and sighed. Drifting off to sleep he whispered

"I'm sorry Betty."

The Edge Of The City

Chapter 2

The Institution

No one explained to Jess why she was at Oakwood, why she couldn't go home or how long she would need to be there, as if it had already been taken for granted that she wouldn't understand the answers to unasked questions the minute she walked through the large double doors of the main hall. With no notion of time, one week, one year, fifty years, Jess struggled to acclimatise and accept the reality of her fate. As the weeks had become months her hopes began to fade. She stopped looking at the ward door every time it opened expecting to see her parents calling to collect her again.

Oakwood was like nothing that Jess, or in fact Stan, had ever known before. A world within a world, self contained, beautiful and in some ways mystical. The long driveway was the only link to the outside village, with the tallest elm trees on either side and the sweeping bends obstructing the view from the world beyond. Towards the end of the drive was some staff accommodation; detached houses like any found in any village. That's what Oakwood was like "not unlike any village," but differentiated by the imposing main hall.

Oakwood Hall, situated at the end of the drive, was the most beautiful building Stan had ever seen; a Victorian stone building with all the elegance and wonder of anything he had known before, with long narrow windows, split panes and sprouting turrets with white painted domes. Large three pointed chimneys rose up from the roof at different heights.

The entrance, for many families the first experience of Oakwood, was accessible between two curved stone pillars under a thick symmetrical lintel leading to large varnished doors.

Through the doors, the elegance continued with the mosaic tile floor, dark varnished wood staircase and matching dark panelled walls. Two benches on either side were where families sat on arrival at the institution.

Outside the hall a statue of an angel overlooked the entrance, but her sympathetic smile and piercingly realistic eyes were little comfort to the turmoil of many loving parents – making the hardest move of their lives.

Most of Oakwood was only accessible on foot along neatly defined footpaths winding their way around the whole site.

Continuing along the main walk was a small subsidiary path leading to the hospital farm. Many of the patients worked on the farm; it was a popular choice for many who loved animals. Limited to only around thirty hens, two goats, a cow and at one point a resident donkey, it didn't really compare to the fully functioning working farm of the "outside". However, to many it meant extra time to smoke, a breath of fresh air with heat from the adjacent laundry taking the chill off the cold winter breeze.

Steam continued to rise throughout the day from the laundry chimneys, increasing more and more after the large wheeled baskets pulled up. With no name tags, no ward labels and no defined sizes, the laundry was not a mentally taxing place to work, the only complication being a separate wash for the red hospital jumpers, traditionally reserved for those likely to abscond, making them easier to spot.

The core of the site housed the six largest wards, while further up the bank as the hospital expanded more units sprang up. The six oldest and largest wards were two for men and two for women and two specifically used for those with behavioural problems, known throughout the hospital as Ward 3. The other four of these wards were mostly used by the older patients who had been at the hospital since the early days. With two storeys of grey looking buildings, the units were quite boxy and chiselled in style, not at all reflecting the elegance of the main hall. The wrought iron verandas now with flaky white paint, accessible from both sides, added to the parallel symmetry of appearance.

At the back of the site, at the bottom of the hill were the nursery, children's ward and the site of the new school for those brought here as infants.

Over the hill were the workshops containing rows of tables similar to any other factory of the time. Here patients were involved in contracted piece work, mechanics, printing, pottery, sewing or various token activities for the less able.

The green painted wooden sports hall and football field separated the workshops from the newer wards which had sprung up in abundance since the creation of the new NHS seven years before.

Learning from the mistakes of the past, the living areas of the new wards were divided by glass panelled walls giving an easier viewing plan and necessitating fewer staff to each ward. On one side of the building were the living areas and central dining room. Three long multi bedded dormitories sprang up off the main corridor and the far side housed the toilet block and shower room - one shower room for every twenty beds.

The wards formed a circular shape with rows outwards looking down on to the central church. Around the paths were scattered stone cherubs, bird baths and ornate sculptured features to be appreciated from the newly painted wooden benches – a reminder of Oakwood's Victorian roots.

Jess's ward was further up the hill, further away from the central section of the hospital but with the best views. Only the newly built nurses' home was beyond her ward and marked the edge of Oakwood's territory.

The central square in front of the church accommodated the visitors' pavilion, patients' shops and post office and the recreation hall where most activities took place, making it the heart of Oakwood's community. It was a real community - even the staff seemed to be married to other staff or have aunties, cousins and parents working on other wards. Jess could see why people were happy here; they had friends, activities, work and beautiful scenery. Not her though, she had a home and this wasn't it. She wasn't like the people there, and never would be. Her life was at home with her mother, reading about mystical lands they had no intention of visiting.

Chapter 3

Richard

It snowed in April in 1956. Night after night the wind grew cold and down came another downfall. Oakwood was bleak and beautiful at the same time. Mile upon mile of untouched crisp snow lay on the adjoining fields, framed by the weighed down branches of the surrounding fir trees. Although there had been some attempt to clear the paths, the weather only seemed to exaggerate the gulf between Oakwood and the nearby villages.

The bleak weather reflected Jess's mood which was slowly sliding from one of loneliness and hurt to one of hopelessness and complete despair. More so at night; that was the worst time. She'd close her eyes and pray that sleep would come quickly but the cold air coupled with the unceasing moaning of certain patients made that completely impossible.

"Night, night," Ruth the nurse said.

She was the only person who had had a kind word to say to her since she arrived.

"Night, night," Jess repeated back. She closed her eyes as tight as possible thinking that might help sleep come quicker. Her mind reflected over the day. Carol had annoyed her. Carol was her friend from the workshop – at least she used to be; now she spent all her time with Keith. Boys and girls were supposed to be kept separate at Oakwood. The wards, the dances, the workshop, even church, divided men and women.

That didn't stop them meeting up. The grounds were so vast and as long as you were back at the time you were supposed to be and didn't get seen, there was a lot you could get away with.

"Keith's my boyfriend, Keith and I are going to get married, Keith loves me, Keith's my boyfriend," she'd repeat over and over again. Keith was shorter than Carol and around double her age but that didn't stop Jess feeling envious.

"I want a boyfriend, I want to get married!" she exclaimed to Ruth.

"Boys will only get you into trouble," she said, "You're better off on your own," which in no way made Jess any happier. Her nose was running. She wiped it on her blanket as she pulled it over her shoulder. Everyone seemed to have a cold at Oakwood.

I'll show Carol, she thought. I'll get a boyfriend. A wave of tiredness hit as the noise seemed further away.

"Keith's my boyfriend, Keith loves me, Keith and I are getting married, Keith's my boyfriend," Carol sang the next day at work over and over. Jess pretended not to hear which only served to intensify the chant.

She had made up her mind not to walk back to the ward with Carol today so she deliberately spent longer putting on her coat. Waiting until she was out of sight, she turned to go the long way back to the ward.

The hill was steep and the previously untouched snow made her feet feel heavy but it was worth it. At the top she stopped to get her breath. She looked at the view. It was getting dark and the snow covered most of it but it gave an idea of the size of Oakwood. It would be easy to believe that there wasn't a world outside, that everything was there.

From this height Jess could see the frost on the roofs of most of the buildings, the winding paths, old stone walls and the steam from the laundry rising until it became entwined with the low lying fog. If she squinted her eyes she could convince herself that she was a princess looking out of the palace to admire her magic kingdom, just like the one her mum used to read to her about. Colin would make a "tutting" noise and roll his eyes disapprovingly when her mum read to her but that didn't bother Jess, he had no place in her mystical imagination. Jess giggled to herself as she noticed the visibility of her exhaled breath, and she did it again.

On the other side of the hill was the school and the yard, all shut up now and in darkness. Beyond that was the site where the new school was being built. She made up her mind to explore.

"Hello" said a voice as she approached the site. Jess jumped, not expecting to see anyone down there. "H-hello"' she stuttered, wiping her nose. "You want a drink?"' She walked closer to see it was one of the builders. He was dressed in a thick black jacket. His hairy eyebrows stretched right across both eyes without a break. A red scarf covered the rest of his ears fastening loosely under his stubbly chin.

Jess walked closer still as he held out the cup part of his flask. Without saying anything she put out both hands to steady the cup. It was warm and welcoming on her chest which was still tight from the cold air and steep walk.

"I'm Richard," he informed her.

"My name is Jessica Elizabeth Patterson, Elizabeth like my mum" she said proudly, repeating what her dad had said to her.

"It's nice to meet you Jessica Elizabeth Patterson – do you live here?"

"Yes, but I'm going home soon," she said confidently. It wasn't a lie as she had no real idea if it was true or not.

"I see," he nodded.

"You're very pretty" he added encouragingly. Her shame melted away. She couldn't believe he was talking to her; she smiled as she breathed into the cup.

Her mum had always told she was pretty, but it never made her feel like this.

"You must have lots of boyfriends"

"No, Carol Rogerson has a boyfriend – she's going to get married – to Keith" she stated trying to show she knew what he meant. Richard smiled as she sipped some more of the tea.

"Sit down," he said, gesturing towards a half built wall. He sat next to her and leaned in close.

"How's your tea?"

"Good and hot" she said rather inappropriately loud. Richard smiled again and put his arm around her shoulders. If felt safe and exciting at the same time.

"Do you have a girlfriend?" she asked – hoping he'd say "no".

"Not exactly," he said. "Do you want to be my girlfriend?"

"OK," she giggled nervously.

"You can't tell anyone though," he added quickly. "It's our secret."

She nodded. "OK" she repeated.

"Good girl." He stroked her hair.

It occurred to her now how dark it was around her.

"I have to go," she said, getting up quickly.

"OK" he nodded, "don't want anyone to find out our secret – I'll be here on my own every night about this time."

She nodded and left.

The panic was unwarranted; when she got back everything was still the same – despite her life being totally different.

No one had ever suggested she could have a boyfriend before. The boys back home laughed at her or called her names; she hated them. This was different, this was real and grown up like her mother and father had been.

"Are you going to be my husband?" she asked openly one night.

"Ha, maybe" he smiled, and she smiled back. The nights were starting to get lighter and warmer again but they still huddled together all the same.

"Where are you going?" Carol asked. Jess had carelessly walked away from the group without checking who was watching. The lighter nights made slipping away impossible. "Mind your own business," she shouted, not really caring if that annoyed her or not. Carol was too busy looking for Keith by the time she'd finished her reply.

She hurried up the hill, realising she was later than usual.

"Where've you been?" Richard snapped.

"Sorry" Jess whispered.

"It's okay" he said pacing around.

"Sorry, Richard," she repeated. He stepped and looked at her, not in the same way as before but angrily and frowning. Stepping forward he put his arm around her waist and pulled her torso towards him. He kissed her cheek, then her neck – not gently as before but hard and fast.

"What's wrong?" Jess tried to ask but Richard didn't say a thing.

As she tried to step back, he pulled her back towards him by her blouse.

"Come on," he was shouting now, "the nights are getting lighter – if we don't do it now I'll lose my chance".

Jess didn't understand what he meant but he was starting to hurt.

"Ah" she protested.

"Shut up." He reached up and touched her chin and pulled at the other side of her blouse.

"Stop it, please, please Richard."

He put his hand up her blouse and grabbed her breast.

"Please, please stop!" Her voice was getting louder

"Shut up you stupid girl!" Pushing her to the ground, her head banged against the side of the bricks – tears welled up in her eyes.

"Stop it, I want my mum."

Ignoring the pleas, he lifted up her skirt and reached for her pants. With the other hand over her mouth muting her sobs he pulled at her underwear.

"Richard?" a male voice shouted. He shot up quickly but it was too late.

"What the hell?" The male voice shouted in disbelief as Jess's sobs continued into near hysteria.

"It's OK," Richard started to explain. "She's one of them, the idiots, lunatics!"

Jess stopped sobbing for a second, not really believing he could be so cruel, but started again moments later.

"Richard, you can't just help yourself!" explained the voice, still shocked.

"Why, who cares?"

"She's a person, she's still a person."

"No she's not, not really."

The stranger put his hand under Jess's armpit and pulled her up to her feet. She straightened herself up and ran, leaping over the wall without pausing for breath, straight back to the ward. Trying not to let anyone hear her she curled up on the bed and put her head under the pillow and cried. Not for Richard, she hated him, but for herself. She was a person, she did have feelings and someone did care, he was wrong, he was definitely wrong! No one would ever let her feel like that again – especially not a boy.

Stan locked up the shop and turned to walk home. To his new home; he'd been here four months but it still felt new. He couldn't have stayed back where he was, not now, too many memories haunted him. So when Mrs Fleeceman told him of this shop and cottage up in Yorkshire he jumped at the chance without giving it a second thought.Not that it had made any difference, he was still haunted. The guilt of giving up Jess seemed to pack up and move down with him.

"What would mother think of you?" Derek had shouted when he'd explained to the twins.

"How could you? How could you? How can you be so selfish?"

"It's not like that; I'm a man, I can't care for a young girl."

"That's an excuse."

"It wasn't right, what would people think?" Stan continued.

"Is that all you care about? What people think?"

"You're just a boy, you've no idea how people can be, it matters what they think."

"Not to me," Derek said firmly, but less angrily than before.

"I'm not going to live my life for other people" he said as he turned and left the room, his footsteps disappearing as he climbed the stairs.

Stan wiped the sweat off his brow and turned to Colin who was still tucking happily into his ham sandwich.

"Don't worry about him" he offered with his mouth still full of his last bit.

"You've done the right thing, he's just had an argument with Martin, he's a bit sensitive."

Stan didn't really hear him, he paced around the room - he could hear his heart beating through his chest.

A door slammed upstairs and the steps returned, this time increasing in volume.

"Derek, I..."

"Don't!" was all he could manage to say. He threw his rucksack over his shoulder and slammed the front door.

Stan's lip trembled and he took a step back. The whole world seemed to be weighing him down like a physical weight.

"How much more?" he shouted. "First Betty, then Jess, now Derek." The weight pulled him down to the bottom of the stairs; his tears trickled down his cheeks. For the first time in his life he didn't care what anyone thought.

Chapter 4

Yorkshire

Life had started to turn a corner for Stan. "Sometimes you have to hit rock bottom before things get better," Mrs Fleeceman had once said. The night Derek left – that was rock bottom for him. The harsh realisation of loss had hit him hard, part of him had wanted to end it all that night, but as the sun had come up the following day, a nice feeling of hope came with it.

Now he'd settled into a routine in Yorkshire. It was a quiet village but there was a close community spirit, not in a nosy or intruding way but welcoming and friendly. The shop was a general store; everyone in the village got their groceries there so he was never short of someone to talk to, not during the day.

It was a new challenge for him. Since leaving the navy he'd moved from job to job, not really settling anywhere, but now he had a focus, something to take his mind off the past.

The boys had moved on too. Colin had a girlfriend – Catherine in Scotland - and was getting married next month. Derek, he had heard from Colin, had lodgings in London in which he planned to spend his leave. He'd written twice to the address Colin had given him but without reply.

The cottage had a cosy feel, quieter than he was used to but still, it was home. The ginger cat he'd called Tommy kept him company in the evenings. He'd been in the house when he arrived and he had no idea who he belonged to, but he seemed to accept Stan into his home so they shared the warmth of the fire. After being accustomed to a house of six people a couple of years ago, he found Tommy's presence really a welcome help to getting used to being alone.

The best thing about his new life was that no one knew him. No one knew any of his life before. A clean slate, a fresh start, it was just what he needed.

One lady in particular, Helen, he'd become quite friendly with. She'd always ask how he was and took a genuine interest in his reply. She wasn't like some of the village gossips, she kept herself to herself.

"You getting something for your husband's tea?" he asked, trying to think of something to say.

"No, no husband, not now."

Stan felt both pleased and a little embarrassed.

"Oh, I'm sorry."

"It's OK; it was a long time ago – missing in action 1941."

"I see." He paused. "Do you have children?"

"No, there's just me, we were only married six months. I always wanted some, but life's not like that.' There was a silence that seemed tenfold longer than it actually was.

"How about you?"

"A widower"' he replied. "My wife died early last year of cancer."

"Oh." It was her turn to feel self-conscious. "Children?"' she asked.

"Twins" he replied. "Two boys, Derek and Colin."

"No girls?"

"No" he replied, quite abruptly. He hadn't meant to lie but once it was out of his mouth he couldn't take it back. "No girls," he continued.

It was late October now and the village seemed to have turned a lovely colour of brown and orange. One day he was on his way to the post office and decided to cut through the park. Helen was sitting on a bench by the duck pond.

"Hello, Mr Patterson"

"Stan" he corrected. "I'm just off to the post office if you fancy a walk".

"That would be lovely" she replied, getting to her feet.

"How are you settling in Stan?" she asked.

"You got used to the quietness?"

"It's just how I like it," Stan replied, "although the nights are a bit lonely."

He looked away quickly with the realisation that he might have just shared more than was socially appropriate. "There's a dance on Saturday" Helen said, a little timidly.

"Oh, would you like to go?" Stan felt he had to ask but it didn't worry him. He enjoyed her company.

"OK" Helen said coolly. "That would be lovely."

"Great, I'll call at for you at seven". With that he turned to go down the steps to the post office. Leaves from the overhanging trees collected on every step. Was this a betrayal of Betty? It didn't feel like it. That part of his life was separate, in a box, not to be touched. He smiled to himself as a sharp wind hit his face.

Life for Jess couldn't be more different. She hadn't spoken to anyone about Richard. The shame and guilt made it unbearable for her to admit it, even to herself. It had been a vicious attack, but it was his words that hit the hardest – they went over and over in her head. *"An idiot, a lunatic, not a real person."* Another betrayal, another person who let her down when she was prepared to give everything unreservedly. She thought more about her mother, more obsessionally now. This was her only hope, that one day she'd come back and take her away from the prison of loneliness.

People were starting to make their way down to the dining room; they instinctively knew it was dinner time even though most couldn't tell the time. Meal times never lasted very long at Oakwood, the plate was on the table as you sat down and most people ate faster than anyone she'd ever known. The first few weeks she'd had food taken off her plate by the woman sitting next to her – so she'd soon learned to eat quickly herself.

She sat at the table and waited for her plate. You were expected to eat everything even if you didn't like it, which applied to most of what you got as Jess thought it was vile, but hunger was too painful an alternative so she'd tuck in. You could buy sweets in the hospital – not with real money but with the tokens they gave you to use at the shop, and if you had visitors you could get tea and cakes at the pavilion.

The trolley was pushed to the end of the dining room. They had a kitchen on the ward but didn't cook there as everything came from the hospital kitchen. The amount you received depended on who was serving up and whether they liked you or not. Today was the mean fat nurse – she didn't like Jess.

"Take you hands out of your pockets!" she shouted today.

Jess obediently did as she was told and sat down at the table.

"Yuk!" Jess said, louder than she had meant to as a sloppy excuse for a meal was placed in front of her.

"What did you say?" The nurse seemed to be targeting her today.

"Nothing," Jess said and put her head down.

"Stupid girl!" the nurse muttered.

"No I'm not!" Jess couldn't believe she was standing up against the biggest bully on the ward.

"Don't answer me back or you'll end up in ward 3."

Ward 3 was for the badly behaved patients. It was locked all the time and the nurses always threatened it to keep patients in line.

"Don't tell me what to do!" Jess's anger was welling up now.

"I will tell you and you'll do exactly as I say."

"No! I will not!" She was shouting now, "I won't, I won't!. I'm going home, this isn't my home, I don't live here."

"You do now," the nurse said, smirking at Jess's outburst.

"No, no, my mother wants me to live with her, she wrote and told me" she lied. "Ruth said."

"Is that so?" The fat nurse continued to smile.

"Yes it is so; I'm going home, my mother's coming, you'll see."

"Your mother's dead" the fat nurse said so casually, as if she was telling her that her tea was ready.

"No. my mother's not dead, she went away," she protested, convinced she must be thinking of another patient.

"She's dead, Jess! She had cancer, how can you be so stupid?"

No, that can't be true, she thought. They would have told her.

"No! No!" she continued to protest.

"Yes! Yes!" The nurse was mimicking her.

"She's been dead 18 months and your dad didn't want you!"

"AH ....!" Jess snapped at last. Out of control now, she pounced like a wild cat, spitting and scratching at any part of the nurse she could reach. She grabbed her hair and pulled her down to the floor, kicking and screaming.

"Help!" shouted the nurse, not smiling any more.

"Help me!"

Two assistants came running along the corridor and stopped in disbelief.

"My god, it's Jess" one said.

He grabbed Jess's right arm but she pulled it free and with one last fit of anger she punched the fat nurse in the nose as hard as she possibly could.

As Jess was pulled to the floor her last vision of the nurse was of her face splattered with blood and crying in pain. This gave her the satisfaction she needed, and she submitted to those around.

Jess couldn't remember much of what happened next, but she woke up in a different room. It was a dormitory, not unlike her own, but noisier. She could hear screams floating in from the corridor. Her wrists felt sore and she was suddenly aware that she was tied to the side of the bed.

"Where am I?" she shouted above the noise.

"Ward 3" the nurse said without looking up from her desk.

"Can you untie me?"

"Not till you've learned to behave" Jess pulled at both arms, but it just hurt more.

"I'm hungry," she protested.

"You should have thought about that before you walloped Maggie one."

There was no point in arguing, Jess could see that now.

"I know and I'm sorry." The nurse got up and walked over to her.

"Right, that's better."

She untied Jess's arms.

"Can I go back to ward 18?"

"Not till you learn, you've got to stay locked up."

Jess got up quickly, and the room started to spin so fast she fell back down.

"Best go back to sleep for now."

The next day they unlocked the big double doors and hungry, cold and in need of a shower she was escorted back to ward 18.

"You prepared to behave now?" the nurse asked on her arrival.

"Yes, and I'm sorry."

I'm not sorry, Jess thought to herself, not sorry at all, but if that's what you need to hear to have me back... The ward was just as she left, bleak and dreary, but a welcoming sight.

It was two whole weeks before the fat nurse came back to work, her nose still inflamed. Jess had a sudden feeling of dread when she saw her face. She didn't need to feel fearful; the first time the two of them came head to head, with Jess looking straight into her eyes, the fat nurse put her head down and shuffled past without a word.

The Edge Of The City

Chapter 5

Pat

Eight years had passed since Jess arrived at Oakwood. Eight years of cold institutionalized routine had changed her. She was harder than she had been; the naivety of her youth had been washed away by the first harsh realities. If you didn't stick up for yourself, no one else would. Despite the large numbers of people in the same boat, there was little sense of camaraderie, of backing each other up. You looked after yourself and as everyone else was taking the same stance, you were careful who you trusted.

That didn't mean you couldn't make friends – Jess had had a few friends; she'd met a nice girl three weeks ago.

Pat had arrived on the ward, as Jess had, with no personal belongings, confused, dazed and frightened. A little older than Jess had been, but with the same sense of innocent denial.

"Put her in the end bed, next to Jess," she'd overheard a nurse saying. An old lady had moved to an older person's ward just last week, leaving a space between Jess and the wall.

"Tell Jess she needs to make sure she's OK." Jess felt proud. Being well known as one of the most able on the ward, Jess had become relied on by certain staff to help with the new or less able patients. She didn't mind; it gave her a small sense of power and value. It helped her keep a small sense of individuality in a world where there were no individuals – only groups.

"You'll get used to it" Jess told Pat, offering a degree of comfort she wished someone had shown her.

"The dresses stay in here, no individual ones, they just belong to the hospital."

"I'm not going to be here long," Pat insisted. Jess smiled as she recognized herself eight years earlier.

"Just till they get the medicine sorted for my fits."

This was something else Jess had become accustomed to. She'd never seen anyone have a "fit" before Oakwood, but it wasn't uncommon on the wards, particularly on the low grade wards where she helped out during the day.

"The showers are in here and clean towels are kept in the cupboards."

"How long have you been here?" Pat asked, not seeming at all interested in the tour, which annoyed Jess a bit.

"I don't know, since 1955." She remembered the year, but as birthdays and Christmas were not big celebrations it was increasingly difficult to work out how many years had passed.

"That's eight years!" Pat told her, seeming a little shocked.

"So what?" she snapped.

"Sorry," Pat said, looking down.

Jess smiled again. Sorry wasn't a word used much at Oakwood – not to her anyway, although it was always a safe one to use to the staff.

"Why?" Pat paused, a little more cautious now.

"Why you here?" she asked.

"My mother died, my dad brought me – I don't know why."

"Don't you ask when he visits?"

"He's never visited."

"In eight years!"

This was something that hadn't seemed that strange to Jess till now. She knew some people got visitors but the vast majority didn't, so she didn't spend much time dwelling on it.

"I work on the low grade wards," she said, cleverly changing the subject – and boasting at the same time.

"I help get them ready and clean the wards"

Pat ignored her. "My mother couldn't cope with my fits, they've been getting worse, I didn't have any when I was little".

"They have fits on the ward I work on," Jess continued, desperate to get some recognition for her achievement.

Pat smiled.

"Do you want to see around the hospital? Outside of the ward?"

She nodded.

Jess spent a full hour showing Pat all the ins and outs of Oakwood, her secret places, things to avoid. She liked her because she was like her – thrown into a world she knew nothing about and left to cope, but with enough intelligence to feel the rejection and hurt of those who had instigated it.

"Who's she?" Carol had asked as they passed.

"Mind your own business!" Jess snapped, suddenly feeling quite possessive of her new friend.

"She's ugly" Carol said, with little apparent awareness that Pat was still standing there. That wasn't something that Jess had considered before, but Pat did look different.

"She's got no teeth!"

"I had to have them taken out 'cos of the medicine for my fits, it rots your teeth" Pat started to explain.

Carol seemed quite satisfied with the answer and started to walk away. Jess hadn't finished.

"Pat is not ugly!" she shouted, angrily.

"You are rude and very nasty – I don't like you, Pat's my friend."

Staring past Carol, holding Pat's arm, she made sure they bumped into her as they marched, heads held high, to the church.

It was the first time Jess had ever fought for someone other than herself, and it made her feel quite special.

"Thank you," Pat said when they were out of sight. "Are we really friends?" she asked.

"Yes, we are, this is the church," Jess continued to explain as Pat continued to pretend to be interested.

The first time Pat's parents had seen her have a full seizure they were horrified. It couldn't have been a worse moment, on the way out of the church at the end of Sunday service. Claudia, her mother, had noticed her fidgeting and shuffling during the Bible reading but had put it down to her poor attention span that had already halted the progress of her school work.

As an only child of a well respected middle class family the expectations for Pat were high. However, since starting school it was becoming more and more apparent that these would never be realised. Claudia hadn't been surprised when teachers had commented on Pat's inability to focus for long on each subject; she'd continually shouted at her for day dreaming herself. Later they discovered these absent periods were partly due to the "epileptic condition" and that medication could help. But it didn't help them, and the fact that they had a name for the horrendous convulsions only added to their mortification. For Claudia, having children was an expectation rather than a want. Having compromised by only having one child, Pat's fits further reinforced any reservations she had. "Children hold you back, Patrick," she'd appealed to her husband with large hopeful eyes. "We have so much already – why spoil all that?"

Claudia had moved to England from Austria as a child and attended a well respected boarding school. She married Patrick soon after leaving school, realising her mistake within the first two years of married life. Having to live with the consequences of one mistake, she begged Patrick not to force her into another.

"I want to travel and see the world first."

"But I'm not as young as you. I'm sorry, it's my decision, I want to have a baby – a son and heir, and it's your duty as my wife to provide one."

When Claudia's period was late one month the feeling of dread hit her, physically knocking her off her feet. The nausea and vomiting that followed confirmed her worst nightmares.

A few weeks later the nausea gave way, leaving only sadness too deep to allow her to cry. She was trapped, all her dreams, her aspirations pulled away – this was her life now, there was no way out.

Patrick was away on business most of the week, leaving Claudia lonely and scared and lower than she'd ever realised possible. Secretly she'd help herself to a brandy from the cabinet, initially to help her sleep, though later it became the crutch to help her through the whole day. No one was around to stop her and the thought of protecting her unborn baby wasn't anything that had occurred to her. The baby was the enemy and she deeply resented anyone holding her back, even something so small and innocent.

She was careful, she only drank enough that no one would notice and she replaced the bottle every Friday before Patrick's return – claiming to the shop assistant that it helped her husband unwind. She kept her secret to herself, and even when Pat's fits nearly tore the family apart she never revealed her suspicions of the source of the child's problems, although it haunted her every time she looked at her daughter.

"I did this," she thought as she watched her convulsing in church. Patrick was mortified. He'd not seen anything like this before, he felt ashamed and embarrassed as he looked at the faces of those around. Some were whispering, some even giggled but most stood horrified – their mouths open wide.

Pat was convulsing, her eyes rolled back and her arms were jerking up and down. Saliva rolled down her chin, mixed with a faint shade of pink where she'd bitten her tongue. Pat opened her eyes to see those standing around her horrified. Her head spun and her mouth ached as the scene came back into focus.

"What happened?" Her voice slurred – she felt wet and uncomfortable.

"You fainted" Claudia said, desperate to get home and have a drink. "Let's go home."

"She's possessed by the devil," Claudia had heard one lady whisper in the shop the following week. Too embarrassed to argue, she ushered Pat to the back of the shop.

As she got older the seizures grew longer and more frequent. Every time Pat found it harder to recover. Within a year the school asked Claudia to take her out.

"She's scaring the other children, I am very sorry. She simply can't keep up now, she needs special help".

Lots of things seemed a struggle to Pat now and just as she desperately reached out for her mother's love her mother seemed to be pulling further away from her.

Patrick seemed to ignore the problem, hoping it would rectify itself. Claudia withdrew into herself, scared to face the truth, and Pat just grew more and more unhappy.

Eventually when Pat reached the age of twenty, Claudia made a decision.

"I'm only thirty-nine Patrick, I could still have a life, but not while I have Pat. I've tried so hard but she needs more help, more than I can offer, there's so much I want to do. I still want to travel, go back to Austria. We could even have another child one day" - Claudia knew how to manipulate her husband - "a boy maybe, just what you wanted. Let Pat go to Oakwood. I've done my best, she's a woman now – please let her go."

"OK." The decision was made. The guilt she felt as the car pulled away from Oakwood was short lived as a rush of relief came over her, and freedom approached.

Stan had married Helen in June 1958. It was a small ceremony, just Helen's mother and Colin attending as witnesses. They moved into Stan's cottage and had made quite a cosy life for themselves.

The more time went by, the less Stan thought about the past. With Colin's very infrequent visits being the only reminder of his "old life" it was easier to pretend it happened to someone else in a different life time.

Colin had given him Derek's address. He'd written to him about five or six times now, about Helen, the shop, Yorkshire, but with no reply or acknowledgement his enthusiasm had dwindled.

"Why don't you go and visit?" Helen had suggested — well aware of his desperation to hear something.

"No, he's chosen his life, without me."

"But it's so silly, why did you fall out in the first place?"

Stan felt a wave of nausea as he remembered Jess's face when he left her at Oakwood.

"Nothing important," he lied.

Since the lie when he had denied Jess's existence, he'd been more than happy to go along with that and he wasn't going to let anything rock his new life now.

He had a caring wife, quieter and plainer than Betty had been, but thoughtful and kind. There was no whirlwind romance like his first marriage, and Helen's cautious contemplation couldn't be more different from Betty's energy and vitality, but he was happy, settled and content.

Helen was older than Stan, only by two years but her maturity made the gap seem like twenty. Often, when she walked around the village with her mother, they'd been mistaken for sisters. It didn't bother her, she wasn't vain, she was decent and respectable. She wasn't a beauty like Betty, her mousy hair was pulled back into a bun under her felt hat, she didn't wear make-up and her clothes were more sensible and practical than anything else, but Stan loved her, genuinely, not just to fill the gap but truly and affectionately. To him she was every bit as beautiful as Betty had been and in no way was she going to compete with the ghost of his past.

"Do you think I'm the reason?" she asked one day.

"Reason for what?" Stan asked.

"The reason why Derek stayed away; does he think you've tried to replace his mother too soon?"

"No!" Stan was shocked that this had occurred to her.

"Well, maybe it is. If you fell out over something small he would be back in touch by now, unless he's angry you got married again."

"Helen, no, this is nothing to do with you, the past is the past and I don't want to go back there but there are things that upset him. He's not like me; he's not even like Colin. He's sensitive and easily hurt. Let's drop this now. One day Derek will understand, he'll see what I see, what I saw then and he'll know everything was for the best."

"OK," Helen said, realising she was only causing more pain. "It's OK, I understand."

She didn't understand, they both knew that, but this wasn't the time to probe further, Helen thought. She was sure that when he was ready he would open up.

Chapter 6

Jeanie

Pat and Jess had become inseparable over the past year. Their beds only a foot apart, they slept, ate and worked alongside each other. Pat's new medicine had helped with her epilepsy but no one had suggested that going back home was an option. As with Jess, slowly she'd realised that this was never a temporary measure. Jess was her family now, or at least the closest she had. She'd stuck up for her on more than one occasion, got her a job on the low grade wards where she worked and told her who she could and couldn't trust. In return, Pat helped Jess to learn letters and numbers from the signs around the hospital.

Jess enjoyed her work, helping on the ward. She was good at it, and the nurses now let her help dress certain patients on her own, which really made her feel important. The patients here couldn't say much. They were mostly all in wheel chairs and needed help with every part of every daily task. It was hard work as there was no equipment to lift or move patients, but that wasn't going to put Jess off. She'd chat to different patients, mostly in a sweet, high pitched patronising tone as if they were small children, but they didn't seem to mind.

Today she was helping Jeanie. She was her favourite patient on the ward as she smiled and giggled when Jess entered the room. Jeanie had no speech and the spasticity of her muscles made her mobility severely restricted, but she enjoyed life. Some days she seemed like the most content person in the whole of Oakwood.

Today wasn't one of those days. Even Jess could tell the difference when she entered the room. "What's the matter?" she asked in a high pitched, squeaky voice. Jeanie's bottom lip protruded further and tears welled up in her eyes.

"Are you ill?"

Jeanie gave no response, but sniffed and sighed.

"Should I tell the nurse?"

When Jess got to the nurse's office there was a man she didn't recognise standing in the corridor.

"Yes?" he said.

"Jeanie's not well," Jess started to explain.

"She's fine."

"Please come and see."

The man coolly strode down the corridor.

It was definitely the wrong decision. As they entered the dorm Jeanie's face changed from sadness to fury and anger. She jumped up and down on the chair and flung her arms around.

"He's come to help," Jess tried to calm her but to no avail.

"Ah …….." Jeanie shouted and started to bite her hand.

"Ah ...." Jess tried to pull her hand out but instead Jeanie stretched up and grabbed a handful of Jess's hair.

"Ow!" Jess genuinely was in pain now and she signalled to the man to help.

"Ha," he smiled, starting to roll himself a cigarette as he turned to leave the room.

Jeanie's arm seemed to be locked now and the more Jess struggled the more she pulled.

"Ah......" Jeanie's screams got a pitch louder and higher.

"Pat!" Jess shouted, knowing she was down the corridor somewhere. It seemed to take an eternity for her to arrive.

"Jeanie!" Pat shouted, grabbing Jess around the waist. Jeanie had stopped shouting now; she was biting her bottom lip. Tears flowed down both cheeks. Pat pulled Jess's waist and both of them toppled backwards. Jeanie sobbed, still holding a handful of Jess's hair.

"I thought you were my friend!" Jess shouted, which made her sob more and more.

"I don't like you Jeanie Archer! I'm not helping you any more." She turned and stormed out of the room with her head high. Pat, a little confused, took one last look at Jeanie's broken face before she felt obliged to follow Jess.

The strange man stood at the door, still smoking his cigarette. His lack of reaction, as they stormed out of the ward, annoyed Jess further.

"Tell Sister that Pat and I want to move to another ward. We don't want to work here any more."

"Freaks," he said under his breath.

Jess didn't hear and Pat was too worried about her friend to react to anything this stranger said.

"Why does Jeanie hate me?" Jess's confidence hit yet another new low.

"I don't know, maybe she hates the strange man."

"Then why did she attack me?"

Pat didn't know what to say, but put her arms around Jess's shoulders as she started to cry.

Not long after, Jess heard that the strange man had left the hospital. Slowly Jeanie's smile returned but Jess never went back to her old job. She and Pat, as requested, moved to another ward to help out. This time, self regulating her confidence levels, she concentrated on cleaning the ward rather than the patients.

Stan looked out of the side window of his car and admired the country views. He was sure other people in the country took this for granted, but the sight of the rolling countryside never ceased to impress him.

He was on his way to London. It had been an impulsive decision and it occurred to him now, as the adrenaline had run out and the momentum died, that this might not be a good decision. Still, he'd reached fifty this year and with nine years since he'd heard anything from Derek, he had to attempt to get in touch.

With the whirr of the engine fading into the background, his mind drifted back over the past. He thought about Betty playing with the children in the backyard, of their day trips to the beach and of family Christmases in that small back room. It all seemed so long only ago now and he knew the memory was rosier than it really had been, but that didn't stop the nostalgic feelings of emptiness and loss.

Betty was the glue that bonded everyone together – without her they'd all drifted their separate ways. He felt a tinge of guilt mixed with sadness. Stan thought little about those days any more – not even about Betty. It was hard, it hurt so much that he'd put it to one side, 'in a box' was how he'd thought of it. Then, as time went on, the memory drifted further back.

He thought about his own father now, and the strained relationship of two men making the best of a bad situation. Stan's mother had died when he was an infant, leaving him without siblings. He had no memory of his mother and as his dad was more than a little reluctant to reminisce. He found it hard to fit together any real sense of who she was. His aunt from his father's side had helped bring him up, reluctantly, having recently attained the relief of bringing up her own children to an age where they didn't need her support.

His father was a strong man, he didn't believe in discussing his feelings, his house was run with rigidity and routine – probably why Stan felt most at home in the Navy at such a young age.

On one occasion Stan had tried to broach the subject of his mother.

"What was my mother like?" he'd bravely whispered after dinner one night.

"What? Oh, right." His dad who had been caught totally off guard, continued to light his pipe. "Err, yes, she was a fine lady, such a shame about... Oh well, no use dwelling on it, you have to make the best of what you have, son – no use wallowing in self pity."

He never asked again.

Determined not to have such a strained relationship with his own children, he found Betty had been a perfect choice to help build a warm family home. He often congratulated himself on having such a close family, where his children could talk to him and he could inspire their aspirations. It wasn't true, he could see that now, any illusion of a family bond fell away the moment Betty died – it was she who held them all together.

He thought about Helen now, she had been so supportive when he told her his plans – a little shocked by the suddenness but quite understanding and encouraging.

"Do you want me to come with you?"

"No!" Stan said abruptly, panicked at the thought of the lie he'd told her about Jess.

"No, I have to go alone."

"OK," she'd smiled and nodded as she carried on with her work.

Now he was getting close the nerves started to show. Nervous about seeing his own son, he thought – that's ridiculous.

As he pulled into the street, he took a deep breath – it had been a long drive, his head ached from all the winding roads. Scared that he would change his mind and go home, he hadn't dared to stop for a break.

He climbed out of the car and wiped his sweaty palms down the side of his trousers. He took off his glasses and rubbed his eyes with his handkerchief in an attempt to refocus.

'118b Lime Road' was the address; he hadn't needed to write it down as he'd written it so often on his letters.

'112, 114, 116, ...' He followed the numbers down the street. The next house didn't display any number. This must be it. It was an old stone Victorian building divided into flats. Stan's heart speeded up, his hands shook as he climbed the steps to the front door. Just as he did so the door was flung open and an older man stood there, appearing to be in a rush.

"Ooh, sorry," he offered as he realised the door had nearly hit him.

"Excuse me, I'm looking for Derek Patterson."

"Is he one of the queers?" He continued down the steps.

"What? I, err…"

"Hasn't he paid the rent?"

By this time the man was on the path and making his way down the street.

"Second floor!" he shouted back, "Just go in".

Stan realised he was still holding the door, so he entered as told.

What did the man mean? 'One of those queers'? Did he mean gay? Derek wasn't gay.

He climbed the stairs, not really giving the past conversation much further reflection. At the front door he wiped his right sweaty palm again and knocked.

"Two secs!" he heard a voice shout, not loud enough to make out if it was Derek.

The door swung open, a familiar figure stood there in a towelling dressing gown, his hair still dripping as if he'd just got out of the shower.

Stan stood shocked, as if a light had just gone on in his brain. Still with his confused expression he whispered, "Martin?"

Chapter 7

Derek and Martin

His confused expression continued as Stan sat at the kitchen table.

"You just visiting?" he asked, hoping he would confirm he was.

"No," Martin said looking down, "I know this must be a shock, my mum took ages to get used to the idea."

"No!" Stan interrupted "No, no, no, no!"

"I'm sorry, this must be a shock" Martin repeated, putting a cup of tea down in front of him.

How could he not know? Stan tortured himself for being so stupid.

"Derek wanted to keep it from you, he thought you wouldn't understand".

He was right, Stan thought, I don't. How can this be true? He's my son! How can he be one of them? The thoughts were going round and round in his head, he wanted to blurt it all out, instead he only managed "No, no, no, no!"

"Derek's at work, he'll be back soon – please stay, please work it out"

Work it out, how? How could anything be worked out? Hadn't he had enough with one handicapped child? His head spun and he had a sudden urge to be sick.

"I've got to go," he said leaving his tea and turned to exit the flat.

"Mr Patterson, wait!"

Stan continued down the stairs two at a time, slamming the front door and down the steps to the street. He didn't stop rushing until he was at the park two streets away, where he collapsed onto a bench.

His legs felt like jelly, unable to bear his whole weight. Struggling to get his breath he leaned forward, cradling his head with both arms. You're so stupid, Stan thought, it all makes sense now. Longs days fishing with Martin, never having a girlfriend, even joining the Navy!

Derek's never been able to talk to me – not since he was a kid, but there's always been something, something he struggled with, something that held him back from being happy, he knew that. Not this though – he never anticipated this.

A dark cloud was starting to gather as the wind blew the collection of leaves around his feet. What would he tell people? What would they think? He'd not known anyone who was gay before, at least he didn't think he had. Maybe there'd been others with secret lives, outside their family walls, but to be openly living with your boyfriend, that was unthinkable in the world Stan came from.

I'm not going back, how can I have a son like that? Colin's normal, what's wrong with him? Maybe this is just a phase, he considered, knowing deep down that wasn't possible. He was always different from him and Colin. Sadder, not quite fitting in at school. I'm so stupid, he repeated over and over in his head, I should have known, Colin must know.

I can't accept him, I can't condone it. He's not my child! Not one of mine! A familiar feeling hit him. The same sickening feeling as when he'd dropped Jess off at Oakwood. Casting aside a child, a child who relied on him, its only living parent. I'm so sorry, Betty, I've let you down – you trusted me, died peacefully knowing your children were in good hands – I've let you down, I've failed you. I failed Jess, it's too late for her now, how can I make the same mistake again? He thought of Betty, he tried to imagine what she would do; she wouldn't care if Derek was gay. Had she already known? Maybe she did and knew how he would react.

His mind drifted back to Betty again, her saintly character. She was never led by preconceived, bigoted opinions. She took everyone for the person they were rather than the label society chose to impose on them. If she hadn't, she wouldn't have married him – something he would never take for granted and never cease to be grateful for.

Betty's family were well off. After she was born, her mother had been prevented from having any more children when her dad died in the Great War. Although she'd been very young herself when the telegram arrived to say he'd gone, she knew that it was to him she owed her determination. After his death a light had gone out in her mother, who seemed to all around to be passing the time until her own death. "She's given up," Betty would hear people say, "it's very sad, very sad for the little girl".

The only real connection between Betty and her mother was in looks. The auburn hair, a trait of the family for centuries, continued - framing Betty's beautiful china features. She was no china doll though, her strength and independence grew from an early age as she learned to cope on her own. Not needing to rely on anyone, she grew up to be an accomplished individual. There was no hardness in her, she felt no bad feeling towards her mother for abandoning her at such a young age.

Fully aware of her mother's apparent lack of motivation to carry on living, she swore to throw herself into life.

"I'm tired, Betty, I'm just so tired," her mother would sigh from her comfy chair in the drawing room.

"That's OK, mother, I understand."

Betty was a great catch, Stan knew that. When she entered a room people would stop and stare. There was a brightness in her eyes that twinkled when she smiled, giving others around no choice but to reflect back her cheerful manner.

Stan had been so nervous the day he'd proposed marriage, still stunned by the idea that she'd shown interest in him. He was desperate not to lose her. He knew he was an unsuitable catch; she was educated, sophisticated and well off, everyone around could see she was lowering herself. Except Betty, she could see a kind man, with little in the way of affection from his father. Determined not to end up like that himself, he was not unlike her. With her father dead and her mother not caring who she ended up with, Stan felt he stood a chance.

"OK," Betty said quickly.

"Wow!" Stan said out loud, making her giggle.

"I'll make you proud, Betty, I know I don't deserve someone like you but no one else could ever make me happy."

"What do you mean, someone like me? I'm not special, we're all equal in this world, Stan – all of us, don't ever forget that."

Those words went round and round in Stan's head now. "We're all equal in the world." Stan sniffed back the tears. She was so gracious, so open to new ideas, so unaffected by the restraints of society.

There was no doubt what Betty would have done, what choices she would have made. Her love was honest and open. How could he let her down again?

The thought of Derek and Martin together sickened him, but the thought of casting away, of turning his back on another of his children, was a pain he already knew was too hard to cope with.

Stan got up and walked down the leafy path. I've got a choice, Stan thought, one I had to make and live with before. I have to sort this out and prove Betty wrong. He's my son, no matter what he is – I can't lose him now.

It started to rain but Stan didn't notice. Too much was going on in his head for him to notice anything around him. Climbing the steps to the large house he knocked at the front door, now locked shut. Sooner than expected he heard it unlock and an older looking Derek stood there looking quite apprehensive.

"Hello Dad."

"Hello son."

"Why did Jeanie hit you?" Pat asked curiously as they walked back to the ward that afternoon.

 "I don't know."

Jess genuinely didn't — they'd always got on well before, she couldn't understand why that would change.

"Why do some people change their minds about liking you?" Pat continued, "Like my mum and dad, it's not my fault that I have fits, why did they leave me here?"

Jess stopped walking and turned to look at Pat's face — now close to tears.

"My mum and dad," Pat started quite timidly as if afraid of what Jess might say, "they're not coming back for me are they?" Jess shook her head. "Sorry Pat." Tears welled up in her eyes. "They told me lies; I don't like people who tell me lies."

"*My* dad didn't tell me my mother was dead," Jess added to compete, "the fat nurse told me. He told me lies too."

"I thought I was different from everyone else because my mum and dad were coming to pick me up. I'm not different; I'm just like everyone else. I'm the same as everyone else," Pat continued.

"We're all the same," Jess started, "We eat the same, have the same clothes, sleep in the same room. Everyone's the same."

Jess looked at Pat who was sitting on the wall, staring straight ahead, her face expressionless. "Pat!" Jess shouted, shaking her. A second later, as if a switch had gone on, Pat's face became animated again. This was something Jess had become used to, something to do with Pat's epilepsy.

"Sorry, I was gone, wasn't I?"

"Yes," Jess confirmed.

"I'm getting more now; I'm supposed to be getting less here."

Jess gave a comforting smile and put her arm around Pat's shoulder. Although she felt sorry for Pat having realised that she was stuck at Oakwood, part of her was envious that she hadn't had a friend like that when she first came here.

"It's OK, you're OK," Jess comforted her.

Without saying anything else the girls got up and walked back to the ward in silence.

The Edge Of The City

Chapter 8

The visit

Sitting in his back room with a warm glass of whisky, he opened his letter from Derek again. They'd never really talked about Martin or that day last year when Stan had visited. He knew what Derek was and Derek sensed that, but it had become possible not to acknowledge the fact without losing his son. It wasn't all he was, Stan justified, not like Jess, her handicap affected everything – this is just part of Derek, a part he preferred not to think about.

The cat jumped on to his knee. Stan stared at the letter, going over and over the first sentence in his head. "Dad, I want to see Jess." Straight to the point and as abrupt as that. "I need to see her to explain why I let her down. She must think I hate her or that I just don't care."

Stan heard footsteps in the hall and sharply shuffled the letter into his pocket. Helen stuck her head around the door. "I'm just off to church to see to the flowers, love."

"OK," he called back.

He'd not even discussed Derek's situation with Helen, let alone begin to explain the existence of another child. Helen was a caring and understanding person but she was also a respectable and dignified member of the church. He couldn't compromise her beliefs because of him and his mistakes, it wasn't fair.

Why did Derek want to see her now? Why? Why? Why? To Stan she was still the seventeen year old child he'd dropped off nine years ago. He had no idea what she'd become. He thought about Jess the same way he did about Betty, part of the past, as if she died along with her mum.

When he'd moved to Yorkshire he didn't inform the hospital. At first this was an oversight, but after he had settled in his new home he wasn't going to stir up the ghosts of the past.

The immense feeling of guilt he'd spent so long trying to shake off returned. The look on Jess's face when he left her – all wide eyed and innocent. Where was she now? Who was she now? Part of him was a little curious but not enough to reopen the past – it was a closed chapter he'd vowed not to reopen.

"Please let me have the address, and I'll write to her, let her know I want to visit," the letter went on. Stan knew this was Derek's way of getting his consent. It was a big hospital, not at all hard to find, and Stan had no idea which ward she would be on.

Why drag up the past? Stan asked himself. Didn't Derek have enough to deal with at the moment, why add to the mess? Was he looking for answers? Clearing his own conscience? Or did he genuinely miss Jess? – they were always close. Maybe he was trying to shame him into finding her, bring her home and try to echo some sort of family values that Betty had built their lives around. That would never happen; Jess belonged at Oakwood, if not back then, then definitely now. It was her home, she was with others like her, that was where she belonged.

Maybe if Derek went, he would let Stan know she was OK, that she was happy even. Maybe then he could move on properly with his life. What if she wasn't happy, what if she was lonely, or scared or ill?

Whatever the outcome, Stan thought, this is Derek's decision. He would go regardless of Stan's opinion, and he couldn't put his relationship with his son at risk again.

On a plain piece of paper he wrote the hospital address, no letter, no advice or words of warning. He sealed it in the envelope and stuck on a stamp. It's up to you now, he thought – I hope you make the right decision.

Derek's letter took four weeks to get to her, having been around the hospital more times than Jess herself.

"There's a letter for you, Jess," Ruth called to her one day. "A private one, looks like it was posted a month ago."

A private letter – Jess puzzled, she never had anything private since she arrived at the hospital, and she had no idea who, on the outside, would write to her.

"Do you want me to read it to you? Or should I give Pat a shout?" Although Pat was a reader, she struggled, and Jess knew Ruth was the safer option.

"Can you read it to me?"

"OK." Ruth opened the envelope, looking a little curious herself.

"It's from someone called Derek." Jess gasped, her face lit up.

"Derek?" she shrieked clapping her hands like a child.

"Dear Jess,

I'm so sorry I've not been in touch before now – a lot has happened. I'd love to come and see you. I've arranged with the hospital to visit on 29 September at 11 o'clock. They told me to meet you at the pavilion for tea and cakes.

I hope you are well and that this visit is OK with you.

Love from Derek. xx.

"Derek's coming here!" Jess shouted, now jumping up and down. Snatching the letter, she ran off to share her news with Pat.

"29th September? That's Tuesday, he hasn't given you much notice," Pat remarked, seeming quite unimpressed with the letter.

"The letter got lost; it just got here" Jess corrected her. "Isn't it great?"

"If you say so." Pat throughout appeared less and less interested.

"Well, I think it's great."

"Where's he been for the last nine years then? Why did he not visit before?"

"He mustn't have known where I was. He would have come if he could – Derek is kind. He'll let me live with him now and you're jealous," she added for good measure. "You're jealous of me having a family who loves me. I hate you Pat Turner! You're not my friend." Without giving Pat a chance to reply Jess grabbed the letter and ran out down the ward steps.

A moment of panic hit Pat. What if Jess was right and Derek was coming to take her away? How would she cope on her own in a place which was only just bearable with one true friend?

Dad must have lied to Derek, Jess thought. Derek would have visited before now. He was her idol, her only true friend from before – he wouldn't just leave her here – he would take her to live with him, she knew it. I'll show that Pat, Jess thought, I'll show her that I have a family. She sat on the grass, while the wind howled in her ear till it stung. She'd waited nine years and yet Tuesday seemed like too long to wait. Looking at the letter again, she touched the paper where the pen indented the paper.

"I'll show you, Pat Turner."

Monday night seemed like the longest night of Jess's life. The excitement, which buzzed through every nerve in her body, kept her awake all night, only making Tuesday further from her grasp. The incessant noise of the ward that she had so quickly learned to block out seemed to be exaggerated high above even what she was used to. She had no notion of actual time but each moment could have been a year. The mornings were darker now than they had been, so it was difficult to gauge when would be acceptable to admit defeat and give up on trying to sleep.

"What are you doing?" Pat asked when she saw Jess leaping to her feet at the first sign that a patient was stirring. Jess ignored her, having promised herself over and over again through the night that she wouldn't 'let Pat ruin this day'. Jess continued to make her laundry into a bundle at the end of her bed.

"It's only 5 o'clock," Pat continued, dismissing Jess's apparent mood.

"Shut up!" a voice shouted from the other side of the room.

Pat sighed, groaned, and, pulling the blankets over her shoulder, turned her back on Jess who was now wondering what her next course of action would be. She wondered where Derek lived now. Was he married? Did he have children? Her mind raced; as long as he took her away from all this it really didn't seem to matter.

10.30am saw Jess sitting on the steps of the pavilion, kicking her feet and wringing her sweaty hands together. She'd had first choice of the dresses today so she picked one she knew at least fitted her tiny frame.

It must be eleven by now, she thought, after an eternity of no sign. She stood up on the top of the steps and balanced on her tip toes. In the distance she saw a figure walking up the hill. It was him. Different from what she remembered – his shoulders were broader and his face looked tired.

"Derek!" she screamed. Losing all control now, she jumped up and down, clapping her hands. Taking all the steps in one great leap she ran towards him with outstretched arms. "Hello Jess," he smiled, hugging her back. He'd been almost as nervous as Jess about this meeting until this moment.

"Come on, let's go inside," Derek prompted. Jess followed.

"Do you have a wife? Do you have children?"

Jess wanted to seem more calm but couldn't stop the overspilling adrenaline levels taking control.

"Wow, one question at a time!" Derek was laughing now. They sat by the window and Derek ordered them some tea and cakes.

"How are you, Jess?"

"OK."

"How is life at the hospital?"

"OK." She dismissed it quickly as it didn't seem relevant now that he was here to rescue her.

"Where do you live?" she asked, seeming much more dignified now.

"I live in London. I'm not married, I share a flat with Martin – we're still friends," he mumbled, a little embarrassed now. Jess didn't notice.

"Oh, OK."

"Where did Dad say I was?" she continued.

Derek didn't understand the question. "What do you mean?"

"When I went missing. I disappeared, what did he say?"

Derek looked flustered. It hadn't occurred to him that Jess might think he hadn't known where she was.

"Well, um, the truth actually."

"You knew I was here all this time?"

"Um, well yes, I suppose – not exactly where, but he never lied to me."

"Why did you not come?"

"I was annoyed with Dad, we didn't speak for years," he offered, trying to change what seemed to be a broken face. "I had such a lot to deal with myself." He paused. "I should have come sooner, I was wrong Jess, I'm sorry. I will come again, I promise."

Jess's confused face altered further. "What? Come again?" she repeated back.

"Yes, maybe once a month. I'll bring Martin."

"But, I'll come to live with you now" Jess said as if it was already assumed.

"What?" Derek replied abruptly "No, Jess I'm sorry – no."

This wasn't what either of them had expected at all.

"But I can't stay here now you've come for me. It's horrible here".

"Please Jess, don't make a scene, it's completely out of the question, I've just got my own life figured out – no, you must stay here."

"No, no, Derek please!"

"I'm sorry, Jess I have to go now."

"No! No!" Jess's voice rose in a crescendo across the room; a few people turned and looked. Derek started to get up, now desperate to get away from the place and back to safety.

"No!" Jess leapt for his arm and clung to the jacket sleeve.

"Jess, stop it." This wasn't the sister he remembered, not the soft gentle sweet little girl she had been. She pulled forward, reaching for any part of his clothing she could.

"Stop it!" he shouted. Annoyed now, he shook himself free and made a bid for the door. Jess ran after him.

"No Derek, no!" she screamed, too angry and distressed to cry. He ran down the steps and across the grass.

Jess crumpled on to the ground. Curling into a ball, she sobbed louder and louder.

"Jess, I'm sorry, I'm so sorry," Derek repeated again and again, backing away till at last he reached the safety of the car. Still hearing her muffled sobs in the distance he started the car engine. "God, I'm so sorry," he repeated. Knowing he would never return, he pulled away down the hospital drive.

Chapter 9

The Seizure

The following six years at Oakwood shaped Jess further. The way of life became embedded as part of the person she was. Routine and structure replaced hopes and dreams and hard cold determination replaced the sweet naivety of her youth. Now 32, she was a young lady, or at least she would have been. Here she was just part of a group where individual differences seemed irrelevant to those in control.

Pat was her release, her family, the only one who talked to her as a person and not as a patient. Friendship like this was unusual at Oakwood, whose underlying ethos was for the most part "every man for himself". Jess knew this and never took their relationship for granted.

In 1970 another cruel blow changed all that. Just when Jess learned to handle her reality, the floor seemed to pull away from her again.

Derek had never visited again after September 1964. He never even wrote. Jess blocked out the memories along with any thought of what happened before Oakwood as if it were someone else's memory. The present was what mattered now, not some dream or fantasy of a better reality.

Pat and Jess sat on the grass after work. "Are we going to the club later? We could see Brian," Pat suggested. Jess shrugged. Brian was all she talked about. Jess hadn't met him and, by virtue of the fact that she and Pat were inseparable, she doubted if Pat had really spent much time with him herself.

The club dances were on a weekly basis and were well supervised by hospital staff, with boys on one side of the room and girls on the other. There was very little contact between the two – even by the staff. Although the dances created much excitement throughout Oakwood, Jess didn't really see why. The truth was, Jess felt superior to a number of those who attended. Some were obviously less able than her or had some strange mannerism. Even in a place like Oakwood there was a definite pecking order, and Jess was particularly near the top. Some of the other "high grades" took advantage of this – but not Jess, she preferred to keep herself to herself. Pat mixed more. At the club her odd looks and lack of teeth didn't matter around this crowd and that made her comfortable and confident.

Pat rubbed her head and wiped her eyes.

"Have you got a headache?" Jess asked as if it were more of an inconvenience to her than her friend.

"Yes, I need to ask for my medicine again." The pain had seemed to come and go sporadically over the past few weeks but then the pain killers made it leave almost as rapidly as it arrived.

"OK, let's go see the nurse."

Back on the ward it was nearly tea time so they stayed inside after Pat had her medicine.

"Has it gone?"

"Yes," Pat replied, now too hungry to notice if her head still ached.

After tea Pat announced that she would be attending the dance whether Jess was going or not. It was so unusual for Pat to make such a bold stand that Jess was shocked into submission.

Jess, who was a little worried Pat would make new friends, snapped abruptly "Fine, I'll go."

The nights were lighter at the moment so Jess had no awareness of how long they were out. She enjoyed it more than she expected to, so the time flew by.

"Brian's not here," Pat said, starting to rub her head again and beginning to sound a little obsessed about her new fixation. Jess started to wonder if Brian existed at all or if Pat had created him out of her imagination, but not wanting to cause another argument felt it would be better to keep her suspicions to herself.

Pat yawned. "Let's go back to the ward, I'm tired and I want more medicine before bed." Jess, secretly a little disappointed as she was starting to enjoy the night, reluctantly nodded.

"Oh," Pat groaned, rubbing her neck on the steps outside. Jess ignored her, still a little bit annoyed that her night had ended so abruptly – but trying to seem unaffected.

They walked back in silence.

"Brian might be at church on Sunday," Pat suggested.

Jess sighed. "I'm sick of hearing about Brian! I've never even seen him – is he even a real person?" Jess snapped, now a little tired.

"Of course he is," Pat shouted, shocked that Jess could think otherwise.

"I don't think he is," Jess sang like a child in a playground.

Pat stepped up a pace towards the ward and Jess let her go. She soon disappeared at the top of the bank to the ward. Jess stopped, looking back towards the club, then back up the hill. She wanted to go back and leave Pat to calm down but something in her made her carry on.

As she got near to the ward she could see staff standing over a patient outside. There was always something going on.

"She's not coming out of it," one said. Jess knew that this meant a fit – commonplace at Oakwood. She couldn't see for the crowd now gathering, so ignorantly walked past to the steps.

"Pat!" someone called in a loud voice. Jess stopped and turned. A gap in the crowd revealed Pat lying on the ground convulsing, her eyes rolled back and her lips a dark purple colour. "Pat!" Jess shouted, trying to push her way through. "Get back!" a male nurse said, pushing Jess back against the steps. Jess had only ever known Pat to have one other big seizure in the whole time she'd been at Oakwood and it was nothing like this.

"Come on, Pat," a woman's voice said, a little more concerned now "How long?"

"Four minutes."

The more people arrived to help, the more Jess seemed to be pushed further back, till she was back inside the entrance of the ward. Reluctantly she walked back into the corridor and sat on the cold wooden floor. After what seed to be an eternity she saw Ruth's exhausted face at the window of the door. She paused and sighed before pushing it open.

"Jess?" She stopped again, kneeling down to her level; Jess sensed something was not right. "I'm so sorry, darling." Ruth bit her lip, on the verge of tears herself. "She had a massive fit; the staff all tried their best."

What did she mean, Jess thought, not wanting accept what deep down she knew was true.

"Pat couldn't fight it. I'm so sorry – she's dead, Jess."

"No!" Jess shouted. Even the actual words *"she's dead"* didn't seem to be clear enough. "No, she's not – you're wrong."

"I'm so sorry, sweetheart; I know she was your best friend."

How could she say *"was"*? Pat can't be dead, she just had a fit – people had them all the time here, they didn't die. Tears now appeared on Ruth's face at the realisation of Jess's denial.

"She stopped breathing, Jess, and her heart just gave up". Jess had stopped listening now.

The words, *she's dead, she's dead, she's dead,* repeated in her head over and over till it felt as though she would explode.

"No!" Jess screamed, "No, no, no."

"I'll get you something to calm you down."

"No," Jess repeated over and over, her head covered by both arms, her knees pulled up to her chest, as if to block out what she didn't want to take in.

Ruth returned moments later with a pill and a glass of water.

"Take this," she urged, prising Jess's hands from her head. Tears now streaming down her face, Jess felt too exhausted to fight. She took the pill.

The next few days went by in a haze for Jess – a mixture of sleep followed by the continued shock on waking up. People were kind to her – staff and other patients, and no one seemed to expect too much from her during those days.

She was broken; her chest seemed to ache with the pain of her loss. She sobbed and sobbed till she could sob no more. A numbness followed, a close down of anything going in or out.

These were possibly some of the hardest days of Jess's life. Her world was once again taken and tipped upside down and shaken. Pat's bed still lay empty by hers, a harsh reminder that this wasn't a bad dream after all. At the funeral Jess was numb. Nothing going on around her seemed to make any sense.

Pat's parents were there in the front row, her mother sobbing and her dad only just holding it together. It would be easy for a friend as close as Jess to feel bitter and resent the apparent hypocrisy of those who had once betrayed her confidence, now wallowing in their grief and public mourning. Not Jess though; she didn't feel bitter at all, their reaction and behaviour were irrelevant to her. After three days of what had seemed like continuous crying Jess's tiny body had shut down, as if it was protecting her from another potential hurt.

She sat with Ruth and a few other patients at the back of the church, her expression fixed and glazed, unaware of anyone around her staring or pitying her. Pat was gone and nothing else mattered any more.

"Were you her friend, Jessica?" a kind voice asked her afterwards. Jess nodded, not really looking up. It was a male patient.

"Nice to meet you, I'm Brian."

Despite twelve years of marriage Stan never mentioned Jess to Helen. He kept no photos and had no contact with Oakwood. All memories of her he repressed to the back of his mind, with the recurring niggle of guilt the only evidence of her ever existing at all.

He knew Derek had visited her, but they never talked about it. To Stan, Jess was still a little girl from his past; hearing about how she was would only make him face up to the fact that not only was she his daughter then, but she still was, growing up in a different world to him. The shop kept him busy; it surprised him how quickly each day passed. Helen spent half her time with her mother, now an old lady, and half preparing flowers for the church hall, so getting under each other's feet was not a worry to them. In the evenings he would read or chat to Helen. He'd chat about who'd been in the shop that day, the weather, his next order.

Helen was his rock, so level headed and calm. She never complained or panicked but took everything in her stride. She was greatly respected throughout the village and beyond.

Colin came to visit about two or three times a year with his wife Cathy and their girls Kirsty and Fiona, now five and ten respectively. The girls were hard work but adorable.

"I always wanted a daughter," Helen confided in Stan one day after they'd left. "Didn't you?" Stan, pretending not to hear, changed the subject.

"I'm expecting a delivery today at eight."

"Fiona's so bright," Helen continued, unfazed by Stan's apparent ignorance.

"Kirsty struggles a little, between you and me I think Cathy's a little worried that she's not doing as well as she should at school."

That got Stan's attention as a familiar feeling from his past hit him like a physical blow to the chest.

"What do you mean?" he asked.

"Oh, I'm sure it's nothing, she just struggles with letters and numbers – I expect she'll catch up later."

Stan felt sick. Surely she wasn't like Jess – Colin would have said something.

"Maybe," Stan murmured. Was Jess's handicap carried through the family? He didn't know, no one knew why she was how she was.

"Don't say anything to Colin," Helen pleaded, realising she might have betrayed Cathy's confidence.

Stan didn't hear her. His mind raced. This couldn't happen, not to them, not again. Kirsty was such a pretty girl; so was Jess. She wasn't like Jess had been; she was animated and full of energy, her face full of excitement for her birthday. Maybe Helen was right, maybe she would catch up later.

The following day Stan's thoughts centred around Kirsty. People came in and out of the shop without so much as a "Good day" from the usual cheery Stan. At four he decided to close early, hoping the change of scenery would make the negative thoughts stop. The cottage was quiet when he got back, everything neat and tidy as Helen had left it. The breakfast dishes were washed and draining by the sink, the crumbs on the carpets were all swept up and the smell of polish from the gleaming sideboard still lingered in the air.

Stan poured a drink and sat in his comfortable chair which had slowly moulded itself to his shape. It was unusual for Stan to drink alcohol since he'd married Helen; he knew she disapproved, although she would never mention it.

The first drink hadn't served its purpose; he still felt it, the feeling of resentment and injustice masking the underlying guilt.

He poured another whisky, drinking it quickly at first. Within seconds his heart slowed to its usual pace. Feeling relief from this sensation, he poured another large one and relaxed back in his chair. His relaxed state altered a little as he heard the door slam.

"Stan?"

"Yes," he replied.

"Why aren't you at the shop?"

"I er, shut early today; it was quiet."

"Stan?" she said softly, as tears welled up in his eyes.

"It's just not fair."

"Stan, if this is about Colin and little Kirsty I didn't mean to upset you love, I'm sure it's nothing."

"It's not that" Stan said – knocking back his third large glass and getting up for another.

"Stan, what is it? Please, I can help you."

He believed her, but why would she, after all his lies?

A single tear ran down his right cheek – he leaned forward towards her.

"It's not about Kirsty; it's about Jess, my Jess"

Helen looked confused. He reached for her hand.

"Helen," he paused, taking a deep breath.

"I had a daughter." He stopped, realising his error.

"I have a daughter, her name is Jessica."

The Edge Of The City

Chapter 10

Brian

In the weeks after Pat's funeral Jess's life was empty. This was loneliness greater than anything she had felt before – even worse than the first few days at Oakwood. Gradually her body had brought her back little by little from her initial trance-like state to the cruel pain of full consciousness.

The strict routine of Oakwood became her friend. Its certainty and predictability gave her the security she needed more than ever now. The staff seemed kinder too – no one pushed her around any more. The weeks passed and each day her pain ached less and less.

Brian had been to see her on a few occasions since the funeral. Jess hadn't been in the mood for visitors and her conversation was limited to "Yes" and "No" replies. This didn't seem to bother Brian; the social norms of "no embarrassing silences" didn't play any role in their world. He would sit with Jess for half an hour or more, then he'd get up and leave.

Brian was short and stocky with dark brown hair. Some of the staff called him a "mongol". "It's because I have Down's syndrome," he'd told Jess one day, almost proud. She didn't understand but didn't probe further. It didn't matter to Jess what labels she or any other patients were given; he was just simply Brian, that was all that mattered.

His visits comforted her but she never let it show, until one day four months after Pat's death. She was coming back from work and she stopped on the hill outside the ward. Memories of that night came flooding back as she relived the moment. The people stood around, panic in their voices. She hadn't thought about Pat that day so she couldn't understand why, but the vision in front of her was so vivid she could have been taken back in time. Her heart raced and her hands shook. She felt a wave of dizziness that caught her off balance and she fell to her knees. Her breathing, at first rapid and struggling, started to get easier. Down in front of her was the actual place where Pat had died. She touched the grass; a sudden feeling of calm hit her. The patients continued to march past her but she was unaware of them. In that moment there was silence. Eventually, when it felt right, Jess stood up and looked down the hill. Part of her wished she'd died there too, but another part of her, the fighter, made her determined to carry on. The same fighting spirit her mother had shown right up to the end took hold of Jess; she'd made a choice now, however conscious of it. She'd made a choice not to die alongside Pat, but carry on and get her life back.

This was a turning point for Jess, although she'd never consider it so. Not really knowing why, she felt compelled to throw herself back into the world, back into life. She looked down the hill. Brian was climbing the bank. Jess surprised him by running down to meet him.

"Hello" he said.

"Hello, Brian." Jess was smiling at him. "Are you going to the Christmas dance tonight?" she asked bravely.

"Yes, are you?"

"Yes," Jess replied, a little embarrassed now.

"Jess, can I be your boyfriend?"

"OK," Jess giggled, and ran back to the ward.

"See you tonight," Brian shouted.

Brian's story, unlike Jess's, was similar to many of the characters at Oakwood. He had never known anything before his time there. When he was a baby his disability (Down's syndrome) had been visible from birth, although in the 1930's it took three weeks before the diagnosis was confirmed. Brian had been the youngest of seven children, and both his parents, Jack and Anna, were well into their forties when he was born. Their initial jubilation at the success of another boy was rapidly quashed with the nurse's suspicions. Unable to make sense of any of the doctor's jargon, they were shocked into submitting to his instruction to "put the infant into an institution". Phrases like the "idiot child" or "Mongolian idiot" were the accepted norm in those days of paediatric services and the expectations of someone with a disability were not favourably optimistic. The doctor admitted to them that in his experience "such children" didn't usually survive to adulthood.

After telling the rest of the family that Brian had died, they packed up a bag of his things and carefully dropped off the "parcel" as instructed. The doctor had spoken, and, although Anna's natural instinct as a mother was to cling on as tight as she could, she would never dare to question someone so qualified and well respected. Even the local priest didn't question the decision as he prepared for the mock funeral.

The community surrounding them rallied around as with any bereavement. Prayers of comfort and messages of sympathy only increased Anna's pain and feelings of unworthiness, inadequacy and guilt. Convincing herself that Brian was dead was what got her through those days of the unbearable grief suffered by anyone losing a child so suddenly in any circumstances. The grief not only extended to losing a child but the shame and inadequacy of not producing another flawless child, especially a son. A son for Jack to teach his trade, a son to help support his parents, to carry on their family name and provide grandchildren for them to dote on. Forbidden to mention Brian to anyone, even Jack didn't seem to ease her grief. Instead her whole personality changed to the frightened, overcautious, tearful wreck of the woman she had become. Her relationship with Jack broke down. She saw the disgust and abhorrence in his eyes every time he looked at her. He blamed her, she knew that; although he never put it to her in words it was apparent in his whole attitude towards her. The doctor told them not to try again; she was an "older woman" and having children at such an age was "irresponsible" to say the least.

"I'm past my best, no use to anyone," she once told Jack, desperate for him to convince her otherwise. "Stop feeling sorry for yourself – we all get old." It hadn't been what she wanted to hear, but she stopped bothering him after that.

As years went by her anxiety levels increased. She spent more time in the house and less time on any household duties, much to the resentment of the remaining children, especially the two girls, who took on the new role as mother to the others.

Brian grew up in the hospital's nursery and later on in the children's ward. A clear favourite of the staff, who weren't worried about showing it. Anna's role was replaced by five or six nurses who seemed to mother him, not out of pity or duty but out of some natural maternal instinct. He was a happy child, smaller than the other children of his age, even those with Down's syndrome. His wavy brown hair framed a cheeky smile and freckly face. Although not the best behaved of all the children on the ward, his mischievous nature and infectious giggle made it almost impossible to react any other way but to laugh.

Brian attended the school (the old one) on site and, despite his disability, amazed his teachers by coping with exercises not too far removed from those of his mainstream peers. His only limitations were those that others labelled him with, and his speech, which even through adolescence was slow and slightly slurred. The staff knew him so well that he never had to make the effort to be understood. Even the other children seemed to follow him in conversation.

He was one of life's charmers, well liked by the female and male patients alike. As the others grew older and taller, Brian plateaued at around five foot, growing only outwards steadily from that time on.

Brian had a stubborn streak, he liked what was familiar and often no amount of persuasion could convince him to think otherwise.

On finishing school, he and another patient Jimmy were allocated jobs on the farm, growing the vegetables used by the hospital kitchen. He enjoyed the work in the summer, but disliked the winters, which, despite every measure made his stubby fingers blue and ache with pain. Jimmy liked Brian, he was popular and he could gain respect just by being his mate. They were for some time the heart of Oakwood's social scene – every dance, celebration, organised activity was arranged with them in mind.

By the time Brian met Pat in 1970, he was probably the most well known patient in the whole hospital. He latched on to Pat when he found out she could read and write, a sign that she was of similar intelligence to himself. Although he was popular, liked by all the staff and patients, Brian had never had a girlfriend before and never seemed sorry for the lack of it – until now.

Whilst Jess's life was starting to improve again, Stan's had taken a downward turn. At first Helen had not reacted at all to his revelation that he had a daughter. She sat and listened for an hour to the whole story. Stan had wanted her to say something – give some clue as to how she felt, but her face gave nothing away – no shock, no anger, just blank and expressionless. At the end they sat together in silence for ten minutes or more. *Just say something* Stan wanted to shout, anything would be better than this. Eventually Helen got up from her seat and climbed the stairs. Stan ran up after her. Saying nothing, she opened the cupboard and took out her overnight bag.

"I'm going to stay at my mum's for a bit."

"Wait, Helen, stay, we can talk?"

She continued packing.

"Helen please, you said I could tell you anything."
Helen shut the case and turned to the bedroom door.
"Yes I did – so why did you lie to me for fourteen
years?" It was her parting shot as she left the room.
Seconds later he heard the front door slam.

What started as a few days away from home turned
into months as Helen's mother's health deteriorated.
At first this was a convenience for Helen. It gave her
an excuse to get away without the village tongues
wagging. It mattered greatly to Helen what other
people thought. She was greatly respected by the
community, and people like her didn't have broken
marriages behind them. It also mattered to her what
people thought of Stan. It annoyed her that he had
lied, but she could see that the decision he had made
so long ago still tortured him now, and for that she felt
he had suffered enough. In some ways she blamed
herself; she'd always thought of herself as a good
listener – a kind Christian lady who didn't judge, and
yet the person closest to her felt unable to share
something as great as this. A lot of what she took for
granted was questioned during that time. Was she a
good person? Did she even care? Had she become so
wrapped up in what others thought to bother about
what really mattered? As the months passed she
missed Stan desperately. The strain of doing
everything for her mother left her exhausted.

This period in her life strained her beliefs further. Her
whole Christian ethos was brought into question. She
loved her mother – but this, this was harder than she
could have imagined.

Although she spent a lot of time with her mother since
her dad's death, followed imminently by her own

husband's, they never really talked. Her dad had been the vicar of the village church, and Helen had been brought up with strict Christian principles. As a family they would read a chapter each from the Bible at bedtime, and the frivolity of dances and pretty dresses or boys was completely out of the question. The strictness had got too much for her older brother Edward, who at seventeen had rebelled, leaving home to find his freedom and fortune. His weakness, Helen believed, was her strength, until many years later when she acknowledged the turmoil that must have caused Edward to go, abandoning not only the family honour, but a very lonely ten year old little girl.

"People look up to the McKenzies in this town Helen, never give them an opportunity to question your integrity." He'd repeated the same words over and over since she was a child but they never lost their value. It was a harsh upbringing, but secure. Firm boundaries helped shape Helen's character into the person she was expected to be. Her mother, though, frightened by her husband's firmness and discipline, seemed to fall apart on his death – as if her whole security system had let her down. She knew the rules, she liked the rules, they kept her safe. Being forced to stand on her own two feet terrified her. This was short lived, since when Helen's short marriage ended with the news that Tom was missing in action, the two of them supported each other.

"You never know, Helen, maybe he's still alive," she'd comfort her in those early days.

"No, he's not, I know, I've lost him."

Part of this reassured her mother, who selfishly didn't want to be on her own again, but she never let it show.

Besides, she knew Helen never really loved Tom. He was the choir master's cousin and although sixteen years older than Helen, was considered a good catch even by her father's standards – and doubtless would be able to instil discipline long after his own death. Ironically, with both of them gone, the ladies continued to build structure and self imposed discipline, as if they'd never really left at all.

Most of their life surrounded the church, charity and doing the right thing (or at least appearing to). Change was difficult for Helen, she liked routine, she liked the rules, as if they were her key to a pure and untainted life. She continued to read the Bible to her mother of an evening, and to uphold the view that vanity was a sin.

Life for her was easier when governed by someone else, and it felt hard to accept that this way was any other than ideal, until now. Now, all this was questioned; she'd always applied the rules but they never challenged her. It never made her put herself out – not till now. She'd always tried to help others in need, but she never let it affect her own life, she'd never been expected to compromise that. They'd always had enough money, enough time and enough energy to commit to various charities and voluntary work without it imposing on their own lives. Now she realised what others went through, now she realised how annoying she must have sounded handing out soup at the homes of poor or debilitated individuals. It had only been a few months but it was enough to make her climb down off her pedestal and face up to her own hypocrisy.

"Come home," Stan said one day in the park.

"I can't, Mum needs me."

"It's too much for you on your own."

"So what do you think I should do – put her in an institution?" This hit Stan hard, she could see that. "I'm sorry, that was uncalled for."

"It's OK." Stan paused. "I did what I did because I thought it was for the best at the time – maybe it was, but now I'll never know." Helen smiled sympathetically. "All I know is I live with what I did every day – I may not think about her every day but it's always there, that niggling guilty feeling, following me around."

"I'm so sorry, Stan," Helen said.

Stan looked confused. "Why are you sorry?"

"You should have been able to tell me. These last few months looking after my mum have made me realise that caring for someone – being so responsible – it's hard work. In many ways it's like sacrificing your own life to care for them. I thought I was a good person."

"You are," Stan cut in.

"No, not really, I'm weak and hypocritical, I care so much about being seen to do the right thing that I lose sight of doing it."

"You're doing a great job, but there's no shame in asking for help when it gets too much."

He was right, she could see that now. Hand in hand they walked up the path through the park back to their cosy little cottage. The decision to ask for help was taken away from Helen as two weeks later her mother suffered a massive stroke and died. The initial relief at not being responsible for her 24 hours a day only made her question further the type of person she was. She returned to the cottage, to Stan, with her reputation intact. No one suspected their marital problems, or questioned the dedication she had shown for her mother. She remained to those around the same respected pillar of the community. It was inside that she had changed. She no longer felt superior or unshakable but human and vulnerable. The guilt of being unable to care for her mother was exacerbated by the guilty secret she now shared with Stan. In many ways not knowing about Jess for so long had been the kindest thing he had done for her. She liked her life with Stan – it was comfortable and settled, she was the happiest she'd ever been, and although she knew it was selfish, she didn't want anything to rock it again.

Chapter 11

The Cedars

By 1984 Oakwood had became Jess's world, as if nothing else existed outside its beautiful leafy grounds. This was home. Increasingly she started to feel less like a number and more like a somebody. The nurses respected her and trusted her with a number of tasks some of the staff struggled with. She was also respected by other patients; often they asked for her help if they were getting a hard time. To those outside Oakwood she was a big fish in a little pond – but to herself and her world she was a leader.

No one picked on her now; she'd over and over proved she was more than capable of sticking up for herself. Those were happy years. She and Brian, although not as inseparable as herself and Pat had been, were close, they called each other boyfriend and girlfriend, but they had become best friends too. Other patients became good friends too, and although there were hard times, there was still time to laugh and joke with each other.

The nurses accepted that Jess and Brian were a couple; they were allowed space and time together. Even in a place like Oakwood, attitudes were changing. New staff started bringing fresh ideas and the right for patients to have a meaningful relationship was now not the taboo idea it had once been.

Jess thought less and less about her time before; this was all there was and perhaps all there had ever been. Brian made her laugh; he would stand behind the nurses mimicking their gestures and expressions until Jess's giggles unnerved certain characters.

There was a new sense of community here. Everyone worked together – most pulling their weight as best they could. The news that places like Oakwood were to shut was not widely believed or accepted. They served a purpose; those people, unwanted outside, had formed lives for themselves within the confines of the hospital grounds.

When Jess had a visit from a well meaning social worker in the summer of 1984, her world rocked again.

"Hello, I'm Miriam" a smiling young girl around 24 announced in a patronising way. Jess didn't mind.

"Hello, Miriam, I'm Jessica."

"Oh, yes, I know, I've read all about you and I have some good news. We've found you somewhere to live."

"I have somewhere to live."

"No, er I mean..." This wasn't going how Miriam had rehearsed.

"Outside Oakwood, in the community – it's a large house with fourteen other residents and they have a structured programme of activities."

Jess had stopped listening after the words "outside Oakwood".

"I don't want to leave Oakwood, this is my home."

Whatever Miriam had expected, this wasn't it.

"But, it's a privilege – you're one of the first to leave here, everyone will go eventually – you've been selected as one of the most likely to integrate successfully."

Jess sat puzzled. None of what this lady said made any sense to her – she used words she'd never heard of and appeared to want her to leave her home.

"I live here!" Jess continued.

"But it's a lovely house in a lovely village – you'll make new friends – the locals are supposed to be really friendly."

"I live here!" Jess repeated.

Miriam was getting frustrated now.

"I live here with Brian and my friends."

"Brian?" Miriam asked.

"He's my boyfriend."

"Oh, I see – no one said."

"I like it here, I don't want to leave."

Miriam looked deflated, as if someone had pulled the plug on her bubbly enthusiasm.

"Leave it with me, Jess - I'll sort something out."

Several hours later Jess saw Miriam climbing back into her car, a different person from the excited young girl of this morning. Jess suspected she'd had other similar experiences with other people and felt a little sorry for her.

Some weeks later another social worker visited, a man this time, to tell Jess that she was going to leave Oakwood, everyone was, but they'd found her a place in a smaller house of seven residents, where Brian could live too. They'd have their own rooms but could spend as much time together as they wanted. An old familiar phrase was used: "It's for the best." Now frightened of Brian moving without her, and losing him completely, Jess reluctantly agreed. A date was set for the move and a number of people visited to ask her more questions.

The idea of leaving her world behind panicked Jess. This was all she knew – the thought of never seeing this again frightened her. Lots of nice people visited, trying to allay her fears – but most of them used words like 'community integration' and 'social normalisation', which only served to increase her anxiety more.

When one lady spoke to her about "choice" and that she had the right now to "choose", Jess picked up a little and suggested that she chose to stay at Oakwood, only to be knocked back down to find this wasn't really an option any more.

She and Brian visited "The Cedars", as it was called, for an introductory visit before the move with five other nervous patients (three female, two male). Jess knew them all and didn't have any strong objections to any of them. On the way there everyone was quiet with anticipation.

It was a beautiful old house, all recently decorated and still smelling of fresh paint. Jess and Brian had been allocated upstairs adjacent bedrooms, with a bathroom in between. There was a small garden to the front and a slightly larger one at the back. The house had none of the elegance and grandeur of Oakwood but it was stylish in a smaller, less imposing way.

Downstairs there was a medium sized kitchen next to a long narrow dining room. It had a large sitting room and a smaller room with no TV, just books and magazines. "This is the quiet room," the tour guide told them. Back upstairs were two further bedrooms, one used for staff to sleep in, and another bathroom that mirrored the one she and Brian would use. There were four bedrooms on the ground floor at the back of the house and two more bathrooms in an extension, for those who had difficulty getting up and down the stairs.

It was hard to object to anything here – Jess had not had her own room since she was a child nearly thirty years ago and this made her feel quite special. Outside the house was what scared her most; this wasn't what she knew, busy roads and noisy trucks, it would take a lot to get used to. At least Brian was with her – for that she was grateful.

The move went as well as anyone could expect – they had a tea party and met the new staff team, a couple of whom Jess knew from Oakwood. The first night in her new bed, Jess slept as she'd never slept before. The quietness and stillness of her room, at first a little unnerving, turned into a welcome change.

On waking at her usual time of 6am she found no one else up so she decided to explore. She pulled on the dressing gown which Ruth had got her on leaving, and a pair of slippers from her new wardrobe. The front door was locked, so she was quite surprised that when she lifted the latch it opened quite easily. She ventured across the garden to the main road. It was very still; the odd car startled her with its headlights. Continuing down the street, Jess examined the houses. Almost all of them had cars outside. A lot had changed in the past thirty years, no-one seemed to walk anywhere now. At the end of the street was a huge building with a car park outside – "That's our supermarket," the driver had informed them yesterday. She'd seen them on TV but was surprised at how big it was close up. In her life before, her mum bought all she needed from a corner shop and Jess didn't really understand why a building as large as this was needed to buy groceries.

She continued further down the street. There was a school, on the outside very similar to the one at Oakwood – now not used much, with painted wooden panels and large glass windows with a surrounding play yard.

Jess sat outside the school on a wooden bench and surveyed all around; it was so different from anything that she knew – she wondered if she'd ever take everything in.

Eventually the chilly air got too much for her wearing only a dressing gown and she decided to return home. Half way back she noticed a flashing light outside her house and immediately started to panic. It was the same sort of light she'd seen the night Pat died, and it scared her. Running up the drive she realised the light belonged to a police car.

"Jess! Where have you been?" a voice shouted

Jess shrugged. "I was just having a look around."

"You must never leave like that – there are many dangers out there and no one knew you'd gone."

"But I always go out on my own," Jess protested, "I don't need anyone to come with me, and I never have to tell anyone," Jess continued, unfazed by the realisation that the police car was because of her.

"That was before, at the hospital, this is different now – you're not safe like you were there."

Still unsure what all the fuss was about, Jess apologised and returned indoors. The police car left after many more apologies and the staff member returned inside, looking a little flushed and shaken.

Things changed from that point on. Rules were made and restrictions imposed. The rigid structure and routine of Oakwood seemed to replicate itself only on a smaller scale at The Cedars and in many ways life was more restricted by the "dangers outside" than it had been at the hospital.

The "choice" once discussed before leaving hospital now seemed less an option than ever. There were weekly visits to the local pub quiz that everyone had to attend because it was part of their community integration programme, every Wednesday they visited the local gym, and Thursday, the supermarket. Those who wanted to were encouraged to attend church on Sundays as this appeared to be at the heart of the community. Jess was given a key worker – Steph. She was a young friendly girl with streaks of purple hair woven into her unnaturally dark locks. She bought all Jess's new clothes, not the sort of dresses Jess was used to and a little less comfortable, but Steph said that was what was fashionable now and at least they fitted.

Many of the "residents" as they were now called had to change their mannerisms. Sandra downstairs was no longer allowed to carry her doll around with her. "It's just not socially normal," some new member of staff said as if she'd swallowed a dictionary.

Despite all this, Jess did settle into The Cedars. As time went on rules relaxed a little and no one was forced to attend the planned activities if they strongly objected. She loved seeing so much of Brian too. She felt quite possessive of him around the other women, but proud at the same time.

After the initial first few months, life was happy for Jess, she fitted in to the new structure better than some of the others, but she missed the security of Oakwood and no amount of "Community integration" was going to change that.

Chapter 12

The Wedding

Most days with Brian at The Cedars were good ones, but for Jess the happiest day by far was the day she married Brian.

He'd asked her a year to the day after they'd moved there – she knew that because they'd just had a celebration tea party.

"Will you marry me?" Brian had asked afterwards in the quiet room.

"OK" Jess replied casually, as simple and quick as that. The staff took more convincing. Some asked what difference it would make as they would still be living at the same place and if it wasn't for Diane, the new house manager, it most probably wouldn't have happened at all.

Steph helped her choose a dress that suited her tiny frame and Diane booked the church and organised a tea party.

In the six months between Brian's proposal and the big day they were visited by several social workers, two psychologists, one doctor and a small team of community nurses. They took on board all the advice offered and even took a six day workshop on relationships. No one else from Oakwood that Jess knew had ever got married, so this made her even more special.

The big day came quicker than anyone could imagine. Jess and Brian had invited a number of friends from Oakwood (staff and patients) and the local Vicar had been very understanding.

Jess looked at herself in the mirror. "Wow!" she said – not meaning to say it out loud.

Her ivory dress was plain and simple, timeless and sophisticated. Falling into a fitted bodice, it accentuated her slender waistline before sprouting into a ruffled skirt which halted at the floor – just short enough to reveal the matching ballet slippers. By anyone's standards she was beautiful. Her hands gripped the stalks of her bouquet which echoed the simplicity and elegance of the dress. The white roses with greenery still attached somehow appeared to be more professionally assembled than arranged by Diane standing at the kitchen sink. Although now 47, Jess had very few wrinkles. Her eyes still beamed bright with the excitement of a child, and her red hair still predominated over the odd stray grey strands.

"Wow!" Steph reflected back.

"You look about 25."

Jess giggled and looked again.

"Brian's a lucky fella!" Steph remarked, clearing away all the make-up. "I hope he appreciates all the effort."

"Can you remember everything from the rehearsal?" Steph double checked.

"Yes"

"And you're sure you're OK to walk down the aisle on your own?"

"Yes" she repeated.

She'd had the option for Diane to try to contact some of her family, but with no address to go on they both decided it wasn't worth the effort. It was all going so well, Jess was afraid changes would only lead to more questions.

On arriving at the church, Jess couldn't remember a time she felt so happy. Although the congregation barely filled a quarter of the church, and neither of them had any real family there, none of this mattered.

The church looked idyllic. There were flowers at the end of every pew and a big overflowing display at the front. Everyone dressed up, some wore hats, Stephen (a nurse from Oakwood) took all the photos and Mrs Hepscott from number 17 played the organ.

Brian looked the proudest man in the world. His black suit had been altered to fit his small stature (no clothes ever fitted Brian) and he wore a burgundy silk tie. A matching waistcoat flattered his portly figure and a crisp white shirt finished off the whole picture. As she stepped up the aisle Jess's smile lit up the room in the same way her mother's would have done before. It was infectious – no one in that room could help but reflect the beaming face of complete joy.

They both of them remembered what to do from the rehearsal, and with little prompting managed to repeat back the vows the Vicar read.

Afterwards they had tea in the church hall with fresh tuna sandwiches and fondant fancies on a doylied plate.

Being the centre of attention was a new experience for Jess and, after her initial nerves, was not an unwelcome sensation.

That night she replayed the day over and over in her head. Frightened she'd forget even the smallest details she replayed every little event twenty times or more. She and Brian now shared a bedroom. They'd moved into Jess's as it was bigger and kept Brian's as their own little sitting room.

Jess thought back over the day – the expressions on the staff's faces, the party tea and the photographer who'd come from the local paper – it was everything anyone could want and more. Whatever happened no-one would be able to erase this perfect memory from their minds.

The noise of the phone woke Stan from his afternoon sleep. Since retiring on his seventieth birthday two years ago he'd spent a lot of his time dozing away the hours. Helen kept herself busy as always with church duties and maintaining the cleanest house in Yorkshire.

Stan coughed to clear his rattling chest and stretched to reach for the phone.

"Dad?" a voice shouted.

"Colin?"

"No, it's me, Derek."

"Sorry son, I've just woken up."

"Are you sitting down?"

"Yes, why? Do I need to be?"

"Dad, its Jess." He paused, not knowing quite how to phrase the next part of the sentence.

"She got married."

"What? Jess? Our Jess?"

"Yes, can you believe it?"

"How? Where?"

"Martin's mum sent us a newspaper cutting. It was in the local paper back there, she's married to someone called Brian, he's from the hospital – another patient."

"Married? But she lives in a hospital!"

"Not now she doesn't," Derek continued. "She lives in a group home two miles from Oakwood, there's a photo and everything – she's barely changed Dad, and she looks so happy."

The more Derek revealed, the harder and harder Stan found it to absorb.

"Jess married? She can't be, she isn't the sort of person who gets married! She's handicapped, and who's Brian? Why would he want to marry Jess?"

"I don't know, maybe he loves her, it says here he had Down's syndrome and that's why he went to live at Oakwood."

Stan was lost for words; what could he say? He had an overwhelming desire to talk to Helen to see what she thought.

"It's great news, Dad, it means she's happy, despite everything, she's happy."

"Yes, I suppose so."

Putting down the phone, Stan's head fell into his hands. Married? Little Jess? After all these years.

It was no clearer replaying the story to Helen when she returned home.

"I always thought she would be a burden, that she'd never have a life of her own but just impinge on mine. I was wrong Helen, if she can live in the community with her husband now, maybe she could have done then. God! What have I done?"

Helen sat quietly, almost as shocked as he had been.

"She must hate me," Stan went on wallowing. "I took away her freedom; I wrote her off before she had a chance to prove otherwise. What sort of father does that?"

His anguish and turmoil only heightened when two days later a letter from Derek included the newspaper cutting.

"She does look happy" Helen offered trying to comfort a broken man.

"Thirty years she was at that institution! Nearly thirty years! How could I? Look at her, she's a beautiful grown woman, how could I write off my little girl so soon?"

As the months passed Stan's emotions ranged between the relief of at last knowing Jess was happy, to the huge guilt of leaving her, to the enormous sadness of not watching her grow into the woman she was now.

"Why don't you write to her?" Helen suggested. "We won't be around forever and maybe she would like to know why you did what you did – it would also help you move on. I'm sure if you wrote to the paper they'd pass the note on."

Helen was right, but after all this time – he didn't feel brave enough.

"How can I put it right? It's been too long – she'd never forgive me."

"You won't know unless you try."

It was another six months of preparing himself before Stan eventually decided Helen was right – he had to write to explain.

Not knowing where to start he got out some writing paper and began.

Dear Jess

I'm so sorry I've not written before,

He stopped, crumpled up the paper and started again.

Dear Jess

I'm so sorry

Again he stopped crumpling up the page and after a dozen attempts, three cups of coffee and a floor full of crumpled up pieces of paper he had a final draft.

"Dear Jess,

I saw you in the paper last year and I knew I had to write. I know you must hate me for what I did, but I need to explain. You need to know why, before I'm too old to answer to it.

Things were different in 1955. In 32 years the world has changed, I've changed. Everyone said it was for the best, that you would make friends at Oakwood, they were the sort of people who knew how to care for people like you. I'd just lost your mum and I was struggling to make sense of anything.

I don't know whether you'll ever understand or begin to forgive me but, I am so, so sorry. I betrayed your trust and not a day has gone by that I haven't felt the guilt of this fact. Some days I tortured myself wondering what had become of you. Were you happy? I see now that you are and I'm glad. I hope you don't hate me, although I think it's what I deserve.

Love Dad."

Stan wept openly as he wrote the letter as if all the grief that had been bottled up all those years now was being released.

When the letter was read to Jess, every care was taken to support her. Diane read the letter out, while Brian held her hand and Steph stood beside her with a box of tissues.

Unsure of how she was supposed to react, Jess just looked a little dazed. She neither wanted to burst into tears or jump with delight. She felt no anger or resentment any more – the truth was she felt very little at all. Twenty five years ago she would have killed to receive a letter like this, now it seemed irrelevant to her or, at least, anything that was important to her.

"Well?" Steph eventually asked, appearing to be desperate for a dramatic outburst.

"Well?" Jess repeated back.

"Do you feel OK?" Diane asked a little more professionally.

Jess shrugged. "I suppose."

"Can I go for a walk?" Jess asked.

"Yes, of course you can."

She left the room, Steph still poised with a box of tissues, Diane still holding the letter.

"She needs to deal with it in her own way" Diane remarked to a now clearly disappointed Steph – who smiled and sniffed as she also left the room.

"Do you want to see your dad?" Brian asked later. Jess shrugged. "I don't know."

"What about your brothers?"

She shrugged again. It was true she didn't know. Her life and family was The Cedars now. All that mattered to her was spending time with Brian and having Chinese takeaways every Friday night. She wasn't sure how she was supposed to feel about the past now.

"Shall we go and watch TV?" Jess asked, changing the subject.

"OK," Brian agreed, happy to move on as well.

Chapter 13

The Marriage

The smile Jess had worn on her wedding day continued for the following months. Her happiness was infectious throughout the whole house. This was pure contentment. She loved spending time with Brian. They'd go shopping, or to the cinema or merely parade around the estate always holding hands.

"Ah" a few patronising people would say as they passed – Jess didn't hear them. Gripping on to Brian's hand she felt safe, loved and part of something. He continued to make her laugh. The cheeky glint in his eyes never failed to make her heart speed up, every time she looked at him.

On an evening they'd sit together in their living room and cuddle up on the settee, neither of them feeling any need to talk. Having spent most of the day together, not taking much interest in staff tittle tattle and with a joint institutionalised background, they often had very little to talk about. It didn't matter though, just being close and together was all Jess cared about.

They'd watch TV or Brian would read to her, often a little disjointedly or slowly but hearing his voice was enough to keep Jess entertained for hours.

"I love you," Brian would say uncharacteristically serious.

"I love you too" Jess never failed to respond. Some nights lying in his arms, their breathing and heart rate synchronised as they closed the gap from wakefulness to sleep. They were comfortable with each other; it was difficult to assess where one of them ended and the other started.

Those days weren't to last as Brian aged dramatically in the following four years, not just physically but mentally too. Simple tasks such as putting the bins out or putting a load in the washing machine threw him. Often he would arrive in a room and forget what he'd gone there for. There were certain evenings when Jess would talk about the events of her day, but Brian was unable to relay his own experiences.

Diane noticed first when he had been unable to sign the cash book correctly; not wanting to raise alarm, she kept her suspicions to herself. A number of new staff started at The Cedars in 1990 and as they'd not known Brian before, they assumed he'd always been like this.

Jess noticed too. She didn't admit it, not even to herself, but deep down she knew she was losing him. At Oakwood there'd been a girl on her ward, Marge, who had Down's syndrome, and the same thing had happened to her - she was well aware of the implication but determined to make the best of all the time they had left.

"He's just getting old," Diane had reassured her.

"He's fifty four!" Jess exclaimed, putting her straight.

"I know, but he has Down's syndrome, that is old for someone like Brian."

Jess had never given any consideration to the future before, but she knew Diane was right.

Physically he'd become more frail too; when he became too frail to manage the stairs, they'd moved into two bedrooms downstairs.

Brian's chubby face grew thin and drawn, his speech became more jumbled and incoherent. His cheeky smile and sparkling eyes turned into a blank, grey wall, unresponsive to anything going on around.

Not all days were the same. Some days he woke almost like his old self, everyone hoped he was back, but by tea time the lights had started to fade and confusion hit again.

His behaviour changed too, often minute to minute. In one moment he could change from being loving and holding Jess's hand to angry and aggressive, looking at her with no spark of recognition, as though she was the enemy.

"Jessie," he said in one moment of clarity, "I can't look after you any more, I'm sorry." By the time Jess had finished trying to allay his worries that she didn't need to be looked after, the moment had past. Brian was muttering a jumbled chant and fiddling with his sleeve cuffs.

Although the moments when Brian was more lucid were a welcome sight for Jess, it felt cruel to him. She could see the frightened look in his eyes at the thought of what lay ahead.

"I don't know what to say to him," Jess confided in Diane.

"Don't say anything. He knows you're there – well, most of the time, that's enough for now."

One day at breakfast time, Jess heard shouting in the kitchen. Brian was emptying all the boxes of breakfast cereal onto the floor in an erratic manner.

"Stop it, Brian!" the member of staff was shouting. "I don't know how they expect us to cope with this," she uttered to no apparent audience.

"Brian!" Jess shouted, convinced she could get through.

"Brian." She touched his arm and tried to reach for his hand.

"Argh!" Brian waved his arm in the air, sending Jess crashing to the floor. Brian stood looking down. His eyes burned with anger and repulsion.

"Get away, get away!" he shouted returning to the boxes of cereal. Tears welled up in Jess's eyes as the whole enormity hit.

"I'm phoning Diane." The staff member, unprepared to put herself in danger, left the room. She returned minutes later to find Brian calm, rocking himself and humming, Jess curled up in a ball sobbing and the kitchen looking like the aftermath of a small tornado.

The doctor came out that night, and left extra tablets for Brian – "to calm him down."

"It's to keep us all safe," Diane explained. It worked, Brian's temper settled, the agitation disappeared, but any spark and fight left in him disappeared too. A part of Brian died that night, there were no more lucid moments, no more affection or smiles. He retreated to another world, with no apparent awareness of the current surroundings. Sleeping most of the day and night, he seemed resigned to his new condition now.

It all seemed so unfair, Jess thought to herself, I've just started my life as Brian's wife, why does it have to stop now?

Eventually, unable to carry out any tasks for himself, Brian moved into his own room. Now moving around in a wheelchair, hoisted from seat to seat and unable to tell anyone when he needed the toilet, or able to hold a spoon to feed himself, he'd lost all the skills he once had.

"People like Brian sometimes get Alzheimer's disease; other people get it too, but sometimes it happens earlier in people with Down's syndrome," Diane had explained to Jess one day. "In the past those people didn't live that long so no one knew that it would be a problem, but because we have so much good medicine now – they're living long enough to notice a pattern."

"It's not fair!" Jess stamped her feet like a small child.

"I know, Jess, I know it's not. We'll keep Brian as long as we can - but eventually he may have to go to where nurses can look after him properly."

"Back to hospital?" Jess asked.

"Maybe, or maybe a home."

"No!" Jess shouted, "No, he needs to stay here with me."

Tears welled up in Diane's eyes. "OK, I'll see what I can do."

"Diane! Promise you won't take him away!"

"OK, I promise."

Diane kept her promise, despite pressure from the other residents, staff, social workers and at times Jess herself – remarkably, she fought to keep him there.

"He'd have a better chance somewhere else," Diane was told over and over. "He'd probably live longer". They were right; Brian died in February 1991 from pneumonia, still at home with Jess on one side and Diane on the other.

"Maybe he would have lived longer in hospital or in a home" Diane reflected out loud to Jess whilst waiting for the hearse.

"Brian didn't want to leave me," Jess insisted, still with the unshaken certainty that all the right decisions had been made. Diane admired her conviction and self belief. Jess didn't doubt or torture herself like most people Diane knew; she saw what she felt was right and that was it – no grey areas.

Diane smiled sympathetically at Jess.

"How are you feeling?"

"Sad."

Simply put but insightful, Diane thought.

"Here's the car now, Jess…" Diane paused.

"Yes."

"I think," Diane started and paused. "I admire," she corrected, "how you've coped, these past few years, you should be very proud, you've been so determined, so dedicated to look after Brian – you've coped with a lot that many, well, most people, couldn't cope with." Jess knew that she meant, people without disabilities, but was flattered anyway – she smiled.

"I loved Brian, I had to look after him – he was my husband."

Diane smiled again and opened the front door.   Jess stepped out, head held high, as she walked towards the waiting hearse.

The Edge Of The City

Chapter 14

Irene

In the winter of 1991, Stan fought off a permanent cold. One chest infection after another left him feeling drained and weary. Helen, now approaching her eightieth year, on the other hand, was like a machine. Hardly ever ill, she led a life as active now as it had ever been. As a young woman Helen had looked mature for her years, but she plateaued at around fifty – while those around her grew old and got grey hair and wrinkles, Helen remained the same as she'd always been.

"All those years of clean living," Stan teased her, "You'll live till you're 150!"

Helen smiled, unsure if she would really fancy the prospect of another seventy years alone with no family around her.

"As long as you're still around with me."

"I'm not sure about that," Stan said – now a little more serious. "My spirit's willing but my old carcass seems to be failing fast."

"Oh, you've plenty of years ahead yet," Helen said dismissively, hoping she was right.

"Maybe, but just in case I haven't, I've written a will – I should have done it years ago."

Helen looked shocked; he'd never discussed it with her before.

"I've left you the house, my pension and I've split some of the savings between the boys."

"What about Jess?" Helen said quickly, then realising she should have thought more before speaking.

"Jess is taken care of, I haven't seen her since she was a girl and she would have no use for it."

"Do you want to see her now?" Now the subject had been brought up, she might as well ask. "I mean, if you really think that you don't have that long left. Do you want to see her, to finally put your mind at rest?"

It was something Stan had thought about for a long time, but more so recently with spending so much time in bed reflecting over his life.

"I don't know, I don't know if she'd want to see me."

"Why don't you write and ask?"

Helen was right – she almost always was. What harm could it do? He had to try now, now it felt right, he had nothing to lose. It had to be now while he still had the strength to travel. Maybe he did have years left, but if he didn't, was he prepared to die without making peace, or at least trying to, with his daughter?

"There's a letter for you, Jess," Irene told her. Irene was a new member of staff – she appeared a little unsure of her new environment, not like anything she'd encountered before.

"Who from?"

"Don't know, do you want me to read it to you?"

"Yes."

"Dear Jess," she began, clearing her throat.

"I hope this letter finds you well. I know how this must sound, but I'd really like to see…" Irene's voice slowed down at the realisation that this was important, and she sat down on the bed.

"I'm an old man now, Jess, I may not have many years ahead of me. I'd like to see you, to know you're OK.

I also want to explain about leaving you and let you know how sorry I am. It's entirely up to you; I don't blame you if you say no. My phone number is at the top of the letter.

Love Dad."

"Wow, how long is it since you've seen him?" Irene naively asked.

"Since he left me at Oakwood."

"When was that?"

"1955.."

"What! You haven't seen him in 36 years!"

"No." Jess remained expressionless, unsure what to think. Irene seemed to think she should be more angry; she didn't feel angry – not now, she'd had a good life.

"Can you ring him?" Jess asked flatly.

"And say what? Are you going to see him?"

Jess looked a little surprised that Irene would need to ask.

"Yes, he's my dad and he wants to see me."

"You don't need to say yes, you don't owe him anything."

"But he's my dad," she insisted.

"Okay, your decision."

It confused Irene; why didn't Jess feel bitter? Why was she not shaking with anger?

"He's my dad," she'd said, simple as black and white, *"he wants to see me."*

Ten minutes later Irene knocked on Jess's room. "He's coming here, January 6th; it's a Saturday, at two o'clock".

"OK," Jess said clearly.

"Are you sure, Jess?"

"Yes."

"You're more forgiving than I would be – after 36 years." Jess simply shrugged and turned the sound up on the telly.

Jess thought about Irene's reaction after she'd gone; should she be angry? She had been once. Being angry didn't make her happier. If she hadn't been left at Oakwood she never would have met Brian or Pat, and they did make her happy – very much so. Pat and Jess had talked about life outside Oakwood once, as if it was a fairytale land. The last few years she'd spent at The Cedars had taught her differently. The world was not the safe, happy place she'd dreamt about. People could be cruel and thoughtless here – much more so than at Oakwood. In many ways she had less freedom now than then. She wasn't allowed to wander the streets alone without first undertaking a danger awareness course and waiting for the completion of what seemed like hundreds of risk assessments. There were no clubs and discos specifically for people like her, and the reaction of others at what clubs there were was not the most welcoming. Maybe Dad was right, maybe he had known and was trying to protect her. Whatever he had done, he was still her dad, and not seeing him didn't seem possible – besides it was arranged now, so there was no going back.

Christmas in 1991 was quite uneventful. Brian was gone and Diane spent most of her day at home with her grandchildren. Jess spent most of the day eating sweets or watching the first series of "Only Fools and Horses" that Diane had bought her on video. Her dad had sent her a card from himself and "Helen," which seemed a bit strange as she'd never received a card from him before in her life, other than the ones her mum had put his name on.

New Year's Eve passed on the same level of nothingness - as the only resident wanting to stay up till midnight she'd shared a small buffet and a bottle of sherry with Irene, who had drawn the short straw to get the sleepover shift.

Stan sat playing with his hands. His mind drifted back to the phone call he'd received. "Jess says she'd like to see you." Like to see me? Why would she? After what I did? He closed his eyes and relaxed in the velvet armchair; his mind drifted back to when Jess was a toddler, his beautiful little angel, he was so proud. Dads always think their daughters are pretty – he knew that, but she really was the most beautiful little cherub he could imagine.

They were happy times; he suddenly felt aware that he was smiling. Her naïve, innocent brown eyes and cheeky smile – the image so vivid he could reach out as if to touch her mop of curly auburn hair. A sudden unwelcome sensation followed, as the realisation of what was to come hit.

Guilt! Guilt like a sickness that only another parent could feel. The same innocent, naïve eyes still looking questioningly as he walked away from her – for good. He couldn't share this with Helen – how could she understand? How could anyone? Unless they'd cradled their child in their arms, overcome by the immense feeling of love, only to betray that person years later- when they needed you the most. What sort of person, what sort of dad am I?

What happened to her at Oakwood? Did anyone buy her birthday presents? Or cuddle her when she was sick? Did anyone tell her she'd done well? Or encourage her to do better? Was she lonely or scared? Or frightened or confused? He wanted to know, ready to face the truth now, no matter how hard it was to hear. Leaning forward in the chair he wrapped his arms around himself, seeking comfort from the hopelessness of it all.

"Jess," he whispered, "Oh God Jess!" He bit his lip as he continued to rock forwards and back. As tears rolled down his cheeks he felt his heart would explode.

The Edge Of The City

Chapter 15

The Meeting

The night before the visit Stan lay awake all night. In his head he tried to picture her now. The logical part of his brain used the hazy photo from the paper, whilst the emotional part pictured the little girl with curly auburn hair and wide brown eyes. The mixed cocktail of excitement and anxiety made his legs physically twitch all night, keeping not only himself, but Helen as well, unsettled for hours.

Eventually at around four, when the adrenaline had completely subsided and the excitement became overcome with exhaustion, he gave in to sleep. It wasn't to last. At six, realising he was in bed alone, panic set in. "Helen, what time is it?" he shouted. "I need to leave early to avoid the rush hour."

"Calm down, Stan – it's only 6 o'clock, you've plenty of time, do you want a boiled egg?"

Stan didn't seem to hear her; he was pulling out his best suit from the wardrobe and heading for the bathroom. Helen sighed, realising that no amount of reassurance would make a difference today.

By seven he was fully dressed and rattling a cup of tea in its saucer as he paced up and down the living room.

"Right," he said, after about an hour, slamming down the same cup of tea. "I'm off." As he headed for the door Helen managed to shout "Car keys" in the nick of time.

In contrast, today seemed like just any other day to Jess. She'd remembered he was coming, "her dad," but really wasn't sure how she was supposed to feel about it. Diane had made sure she was on shift, to satisfy her own curiosity if she was really honest but also, she justified to herself, to provide support to Jess. Jess's laid back attitude had surprised her already. She hadn't got up till gone nine and then presented herself in the kitchen looking like a uni student with her first hangover.

"Good morning!" Diane had said, trying to get some reaction.

"Urgh," Jess mumbled, getting the milk out of the fridge.

"I've run the bath, big day today."

"My dad's coming today," Jess informed her.

"I know, best get yourself cleaned up."

"I'll have breakfast first," Jess said through a stifled yawn.

"OK." Diane tried to copy her laid back attitude and left the room before her body language gave her away.

Despite putting on the first clean item in her wardrobe and slapping on the very minimum excuse for make up, Jess looked good.

At 1.36, 24 minutes early, the doorbell rang and for the first time that day Jess felt nervous.

From the top of the stairs she could see Diane opening the front door.

"Hello, Mr Patterson?"

"Yes."

"Come in."

Jess felt herself gasp out loud as an old man with thin white hair and a walking stick entered the hall. Hoping he hadn't heard, she brushed down the crumbs from her dinner and put her hair behind her ears.

Thinking of her dad as an old man felt strange to Jess. She knew that he would have changed – got older, but this was not what she'd expected at all.

Coming down the stairs, Stan's small talk ended abruptly as Jess caught his eye. The sun shone through the landing windows, catching the right side of her face and highlighting her auburn hair. Nothing could have prepared him for this. His heart beat so loud and fast, he opened his mouth but no words came out. Jess rescued the situation.

"Hello, Dad."

"Hello," Stan managed to produce, his dry mouth still hanging open. He hadn't expected to feel liked this. In many ways she was a stranger, she certainly wasn't the seventeen year old he left at Oakwood and yet there was a connection that left him breathless. A combination of his little angel and the ghost of Betty stood before him.

"Can I take your coat?" Diane offered, interrupting an awkward silence that Stan appeared to be unaware of.

"Yes, certainly." Stan pulled himself back to reality.

"Come in to the conservatory," Jess said a little inappropriately abrupt – Stan followed.

"I'll make some tea." Diane shuffled off towards the kitchen.

Jess and Stan were still sitting in silence when Diane arrived with the tray of tea.

"You have a beautiful home," he said eventually.

"Thank you," Jess answered politely.

"Helen, er, my wife, and I have a two bedroom cottage in Yorkshire, it's cosy but not very stylish."

Jess smiled as Diane poured her a cup of tea.

"Tea?"

"Thank you," Stan nodded.

Diane left the room.

"You look well," Stan remarked honestly.

"I am well, I miss Brian but Diane says that I've coped well." Jess looked proud of herself.

"Yes, I was sorry to hear about Brian. I've not been so well, chest infections one after another."

"I'm sorry."

"You're sorry? You have nothing to be sorry about Jessica. *I'm* sorry – very sorry..."

"Is it because you left me at Oakwood?" Jess enquired very matter of factly, not meaning to sound sarcastic in any way.

"Yes, and because I never came back."

"You didn't visit me."

"I know. This may be hard to understand, but the guilt I felt after leaving you stopped me going back. It's selfish, I know but I couldn't bear to see you hating me."

"I don't hate you, but I was angry. I was angry when I found out Mum was dead and that you weren't coming back. It took a long time to work it out and cope with it."

Stan's head dropped. He'd forgotten Jess hadn't been told about her mum when he left her.

"Did they tell you after I'd gone – about Betty, er, your mum?"

"No, the fat nurse told me months later – she said I was stupid not to have known before."

"Oh God, I'm sorry. Was it..." Stan started, knowing he was frightened to hear the reply. "Was it awful at Oakwood?"

"No," Jess was quick to reply.

"I hated it at first, but then I made friends. Pat was my friend. I miss her too. I had a job – I helped with low grades and we had dances and parties and that's where I met Brian. Oakwood was my home, I miss it sometimes. At Oakwood I could wander around wherever I wanted, the staff and some of the patients liked me".

This revelation felt as though a physical load had been lifted off Stan's shoulder.

"Really? So you weren't unhappy, not all the time?"

"No, of course not. Only at first and again when Pat died – she had a seizure. I met Brian at her funeral."

"The staff told me on the phone that Brian had died."

"He was very poorly, I looked after him. Diane says I looked after him very well. I loved Brian."

"Yes, yes I'm sure. It's not easy when someone you love dies; I still miss your mum even now."

Jess smiled at the thought of her mum. It was a memory she didn't dwell on much now.

"You look like her, very much so – she was beautiful." Jess had never thought of herself as beautiful before but appreciated the compliment.

"Jess, after I moved to Yorkshire, I tried to forget about Betty and you. The memories hurt so much, I wanted to get away. I thought that a new start would help so I pushed the memories to the back of my mind and started again. Derek and Colin lived away, so there were no reminders – it was as if you'd died with your mum."

"But I didn't die," Jess said simply, looking puzzled. "I was alive and living at Oakwood"

"I know, I know." Stan realised this was too hard for Jess to take in. "And I'm sorry that I didn't think about that then."

"Everyone said it was for the best, you'd be with others like..." he paused; "Well, like you, no one would pick on you there and you'd be well looked after. Mrs. Fleeceman said it wasn't right for me to look after a young girl."

"I don't need to be looked after, I look after myself," Jess snapped defensively. Mrs Fleeceman wasn't a name she'd heard in a long time but she hadn't forgotten her – she'd been kind to her when her mum was ill – another person she trusted that had betrayed her.

"Yes, I know you do, I can see that now, to be honest I didn't realise that you would ... do so well. You're an amazing person Jess; just like your mum. Despite your weak father, you've achieved and coped with so much. I am so proud of you. I'm as proud of you as I am ashamed of myself."

Jess softened now and smiled – she felt a warm glow.

"I didn't forget, Jess, despite my best efforts – all those years I never forgot. I thought about you all the time and the guilt followed me around – I couldn't shift that. I worried that you were lonely or scared."

"I was lonely and scared but most of the time I was happy. People were kind at Oakwood, without it I wouldn't have met Brian, Pat or Diane."

Jess's comfort and grace only heightened Stan's admiration for her. After her diagnosis, for years he'd grieved for the daughter he thought he would never have, only to stand before her now, an accomplished, remarkable lady – who despite his weak, uncaring betrayal held no grudge or hatred towards him.

"You are such a strong person, much more so than me. I'm sorry I didn't believe in you then – I hope one day you'll forgive me."

"I forgave you a long time ago," Jess smiled, pouring more tea and helping herself to a Jaffa cake.

"Tell me about Helen."

By the time Diane returned for the tray, the two of them were like old friends.

"I'd better be going, come and visit us?" Stan suggested – not really what he'd planned to say.

"OK, I have your phone number so I'll stay in touch."

Putting on his coat, Stan turned to his daughter.

"Thank you, thank you for making this so easy. I'm so pleased you're OK and so proud of what you've become. Good bye."

"Bye." Smiling, feeling more proud and confident in herself than ever before, Jess closed the door on her dad.

Chapter 16

Caroline

Jess kept her word to keep in touch and, with Diane's help, wrote to her dad twice – signing it herself. He wrote back with stories about Colin's children and Derek's career. It was good to have something beyond The Cedars since Brian died.

Another social worker visited in the summer with yet another great plan.

"Jess, I'm Caroline," she said in the familiar patronising way of the others before her.

"Hello, Caroline."

"Hi, Jess. We've carried out a functional assessment and feel you have done so well, you could have your own flat." Diane sat in the corner of the room and rolled her eyes. "What?" Jess was taken aback. "You want me to leave The Cedars?"

"Well, yes, this sort of house was all very well when we were closing down hospitals but things have moved on since then."

"The new idea is to give people independence. You wouldn't be completely alone; someone would come in for an hour a day to help with your money and housework."

It was too much for Jess to take in. "I don't want to live on my own, I'd get lonely."

"But you have such a lot of ability – you could manage, no problem."

"Could you manage to live on your own?" Jess threw back to Caroline, totally knocking her off course.

"Well, yes, I suppose."

"And do you?"

"Well, no. I live with my boyfriend."

Diane laughed out loud. "I think what Jess means is that just because you're capable of living on your own doesn't mean you have to."

Caroline felt deflated but took her point. "It's just that we're encouraging people to be independent – it's in their best interests."

"But you told me it was in my best interests to live in a hospital and then you told me it was in my best interests to live at The Cedars – were you wrong then?"

"I er, I don't know – that was before my time. You passed our assessment with flying colours, we know you could manage now."

"Now!" Diane felt the anger welling up. "She hasn't changed, your system has, new government ideas, that's what changed."

Caroline felt defensive – "It won't matter to you anyway if you're retiring."

"Retiring?" Jess asked.

Caroline bit her lip.

"Who's retiring?"

Diane's face fell.

"Jess – I was going to tell you, I'm sorry. I'm nearly sixty, I'm thinking about the end of the year."

Jess was speechless as Caroline made a hasty exit from an obviously sticky situation.

"Sorry," she managed to say as she left the room. "I'll see myself out." The others ignored her.

Jess stared at Diane. "Why didn't you tell me that you were leaving?"

"I'm sorry, things were going so well for you, being back in touch with your dad. I wanted that well established before I went."

Jess looked confused, "Did you think I needed them to look after me with you not there to do it?"

"No!" Diane snapped.

"Jess, you don't need someone to take care of you, you can do that yourself."

"You should have told me you were leaving."

"I know, but it wasn't the right time and I had to check..." Diane paused.

"Check? What do you mean?"

Diane paused and rubbed her forehead. "It's just an idea, it may not be possible."

Jess was more confused than ever. "What idea?"

"When I retire, when we retire – Alan and me, we've looked into fostering."

"You're going to have children?" Jess asked.

"No, fostering adults."

"Why do adults get fostered?"

"Adults with disabilities, learning disabilities."

Jess leaned back in her chair, still interested.

"Jess, I've had my checks and been given the go ahead to foster adults."

"Congratulations."

"I, well we, we're going to ask social services about fostering you." Diane looked down at the floor nervously.

"It's your choice though, you can stay here or get a flat like Caroline suggested, but if social services give us the go ahead, it's an option – it's up to you."

Jess was speechless. "You want me to live with you?" she clarified.

"Me and Alan, yes – but it's your decision. I won't be offended if you say no."

"Could I have my own room?"

"Of course." Diane brightened at the thought that Jess was considering the idea. "And you can go out as often as you like."

Jess smiled as though a light had gone on in her head.

"OK," she stated.

"OK?"

"Yes, OK, I'd like to live with you and Alan please."

"OK, well as I said we need to check – but good, I'm pleased you like the idea."

She did like the idea. Diane didn't live far away so she could still see her friends and Alan was a kind quiet man – she'd always liked him.

"I'll do the dishes," Jess suggested, picking up the tray and leaving a slightly worried Diane in the conservatory.

The move was a lot less complicated and more rapid than Diane had thought. Jess was able to say what she wanted and the necessary checks were already complete.

Sandra, from downstairs, also moving to Diane's, took a lot longer to settle as she was unable to tell the social worker what her views were. Despite picture cards, photos, signing and an over enthusiastic advocate's attempt at exaggerated mime, the idea still didn't quite seem clear to her although it did give six residents, fourteen staff and two relatives something to laugh about over the festive season.

By early February 1993 both girls had settled into their new home. Jess didn't mind that Sandra had no speech; she was used to that and she enjoyed helping her with most activities.

Sandra was younger than Jess, in her early forties. Like most people at Oakwood there appeared to be no reason, no diagnosis for her severe disabilities, it was just the way she was. She still saw her mum and dad regularly; despite the years she'd spent at Oakwood, they continued to visit. Unlike Jess, the idea of being angry that she had been left or wondering when she'd go home was not something that appeared to distress her and, if it did, she was not able to express it. Sandra seemed content most of the time to potter around with her doll. She had been given a downstairs room at Diane's as her unsteady gait and unpredictable seizures left her a potential risk with stairs.

Jess's room was on the third floor of the three storey Victorian terrace, above Diane and Alan's room and the guest room. She loved it; with the extra flight of stairs the whole floor was practically hers, as if she had her own flat, but there were still others around when she wanted company. She had a large bedroom, a double bed with a brass headboard and two large old-fashioned wardrobes. Opposite the bed was the skylight window – the only source of natural light in the room. This had worried the inspector who visited but Jess convinced him it was just what she wanted. The pink rug on the floor and velvet cushions on the bed gave it a warm and cosy feel.

The move had led to a complete review of Jess's "life plan" and it was felt that Jess would increase her independence by getting a job at the local supermarket. She didn't mind this at all; although at 55 she'd never had a proper job before, she wasn't afraid of hard work. With a support worker for the first couple of weeks she settled well into the new role of assistant plate washer in the store's canteen.

In the evening she'd either be at her drama group, the pub quiz or calling at The Cedars to say hello to her friends, and on one of her days off she'd started a reading and writing class at the local library and community centre. "It's never too late to learn," Caroline had told her.

The activity that she most enjoyed however was meeting with the advocacy group on Friday mornings. Being the most articulate service user there, she enjoyed people listening to her opinions with genuine interest. It was not something she'd had much experience of and it was a good feeling.

The days passed quickly in those months. She had been two years in her new home before she had a chance to reflect.

That was when she received a letter – not from her dad, from Derek.

Chapter 17

The Family

"Would you like some help in reading that, love?" Alan asked her.

"No, it's OK," Jess said, now confident that most words made sense.

After a couple of minutes she returned to the living room looking glazed – the letter hanging between her fingers.

"Jess?" Diane asked quietly.

"My dad's died," Jess said, looking straight ahead.

"Dead? Are you sure?" Diane shook herself, realising how ridiculous that sounded.

"Let me see the letter" Alan took control – taking the letter.

"Well?" - Diane asked impatiently after the longest two minutes of anyone's life.

"I'm so sorry," Alan said as the tears welled up in Jess's eyes.

"It's not fair!" Jess snapped like a teenager who had been grounded.

"It says he had pneumonia twice last year and after a third bout this year, he just gave up."

Jess didn't know about this. His letters had been slower to arrive but she was too caught up in her busy life to stop and consider why.

Diane instinctively reached out and pulled her close.

"At least you met him again – cleared the air." That made no difference to her now as she sobbed into Diane's chest.

"But he was my only family."

"No, he's not," Alan corrected, "Derek says here that he'd like you to go to the funeral – he says it would be good to see you again – that sounds like family too."

"When's the funeral?" Diane asked, realising it must be soon.

"On Tuesday."

"Can I go?" asked Jess, muffling her sobs. "Will you drive me?"

"Of course I will. Alan will need to stay here for Sandra getting back from the centre – but I'll come with you."

Jess sniffed. Occasionally life seemed so unfair, and at other times she just wanted to crack on and make the best of it. This seemed like the first.

The funeral at the crematorium was packed with people from the local village.

"Your dad must have been very popular, the chapel is full."

Jess nodded, looking around to see if she could see her brother.

"The family usually enter behind the coffin," Diane reminded her – bringing back memories of Brian's and Pat's funerals. Jess nodded. I am family, she thought to herself as the organ started to play. The sight of the coffin made her feel sick again at the injustice of it all – but the feeling soon gave way to her curiosity as to who was following.

An elderly lady with a long grey coat and black hat followed first, linking a middle aged, grey and slightly overweight Derek. Colin was just behind with another lady. Even at this age they looked identical, but Jess could still tell them apart with no effort at all.

Behind Colin and a lady she assumed was Catherine were two very pretty girls, probably in their twenties. One of them was sobbing into her handkerchief as she walked.

Jess didn't take in most of the ceremony as she was interested in looking over everyone's heads to Derek and Helen, but being only five foot tall this was not an easy task, and the people in the row in front started to stare at her.

She hadn't needed to worry as the family stood at the chapel door to shake hands with the congregation on the way out. First in the line was Colin, followed by Derek and then Helen.

"Thank you for coming," Colin recited to everyone walking past, not knowing who everyone was. He continued the same with Jess, but despite looking straight into her eyes there was no spark of recognition.

"Thank you for coming," he repeated.

Jess smiled and turned to Derek.

"Thank you," he paused "Jess?"

"Hello, Derek."

Colin broke off from his insincere chanting.

He turned and looked at the beautiful, well dressed lady before him.

"Jess?" Colin repeated back.

"Yes," she replied.

"I er, I didn't know you were coming," Colin managed to mutter – still shaking hands with people he now wasn't even looking at.

"We're having coffee and sandwiches back at our house," Helen said, trying to rescue the situation, "Please come."

Jess smiled and nodded as she shook hands with Helen and moved out of the way.

"You really threw them," Diane said in the car on the way to Helen's house.

"Yes, I think I did."

"And I have to say, you've aged better than either of them." Diane gave Jess a knowing smile.

"I look like my mum," Jess said, repeating what her dad had told her.

There weren't so many people at the house, just family and a few others Jess didn't recognise.

"Jess!" Derek shouted, bounding over, "You remember Martin?"

"Yes." She hadn't remembered him being so bald or overweight but she kept that to herself.

"How are you?"

"I'm OK," Jess said.

"Dad told me all about your new house and your job and about Diane."

"This is Diane," Jess cut in, realising she was feeling isolated.

"Hi," he smiled.

"I was sorry to hear about Brian – it must have been really difficult."

"Yes, it was, but it was a long time ago – I'm OK now."

Derek smiled again, staring at her. Jess felt conscious of this, and he realised his mistake.

"Sorry, I er can't get over how much you look like mum."

"I have her spirit too," Jess said, again repeating her dad's words, not really understanding their meaning.

Derek laughed, "I'm sure you do."

"Jess?" Derek's eyes hit the floor. "Jess, that day I visited you at Oakwood…"

"It's OK," Jess cut in.

"I was having such a hard time myself - coming out as gay… Do you know what 'gay' means?"

"Of course I do."

"Well, it wasn't like it is now. I had death threats and beatings from anyone who worked it out."

"It's OK," Jess repeated, "I know that it would have been difficult."

Feeling more relieved, Derek offered to get them another cup of tea. The house was exactly as Jess had imagined – not unlike the one they had grown up in, but smaller.

"Can I come and visit sometime?" Derek asked, then feeling he'd jumped the gun a little, added "Martin and I are in the process of moving back home, so we wouldn't be far from you. I'd like to keep in touch."

"I'd like to keep in touch too," Jess confirmed.

"Great, and Jess, thanks for making this so easy." His words, exactly the same words her dad had used, made her smile.

"It's OK."

Chapter 18

The Conference

Life continued to be just as busy as before after Jess returned home. Derek did visit a couple of months later and even took Jess out for a meal. After the initial awkwardness their relationship took a natural turn back to how it was when they were children.

As with his father, Derek also admitted that he hadn't expected Jess to grow up to be the smart, articulate, beautiful woman that she was – which made her feel the proudest she'd ever felt. Her confidence grew to new heights. Her opinion mattered at home, to Derek, at advocacy and even at work. "You're one of the team here, Jess," her boss had told her, "Just like everyone else."

Perhaps the proudest moment for Jess was the day the advocacy group asked her to give a presentation to a group of three hundred health and social care professionals. She was so proud to be asked that the thought of stage fright never entered her head until the morning of the conference. Seeing three hundred empty seats on arrival at the hotel conference room made her stomach do a full somersault.

"Wow!" Jess said out loud to Diane and Derek, who'd been happy to come for extra support.

"Are you going to be OK?"

"Wow!" Jess repeated.

"Of course she is," said Diane, desperate to bring Jess back to reality.

"Wow!" Jess said again, taking her seat at the front.

"Does she have it written down?" Derek whispered to Diane.

"No, reading would slow her down. She knows what she wants to say, she'll be OK."

Derek smiled, hoping she was right, but his lack of confidence make his own hands shake more than Jess's.

The presenter announced Jess in a slightly patronising way, as if they had to be seen to include disabled people so she was a good as any other – but her speech made him think again. In fact it made the whole audience think again.

"Hi, my name is Jessica Elizabeth Patterson. I want to tell you about my life. I was born in 1936. I have twin brothers. When I was seventeen my mother died of cancer and my dad couldn't cope so I went to live in a hospital – Oakwood hospital.

I was angry that I was left there. Everyone said it was for the best - no one asked me what I wanted, no one realised I could tell them. I helped look after the low grades (we're not allowed to call them that now). They were more disabled than me and I made lots of friends. My best friend was called Pat – she died of a seizure in 1970 - that made me very sad and lonely. That's when I met Brian. I loved Brian and Oakwood became my home. I was happy again, until someone else told me it was in my best interests to leave Oakwood and go to

The Cedars. Again, no one asked me what I wanted, they still didn't realise I could tell them.

When I married Brian, lots of people thought it was a stupid idea. They thought that I wasn't capable of being a wife. Brian became ill, he had Down's syndrome and that made him get a disease called Alzheimer's. I looked after him at home until he died. Then people started to realise I was capable of doing lots of things.

Another worker visited me a few years ago to tell me it was in my best interests to live alone – I didn't want to live alone.

Everyone says people have choices, but the big choices were always made for me.

Now I have a job, a nice house, I can read and write, I've cared for my dying husband and spoken at a large conference.

Now people realise that I am capable of making choices – even big ones. This is my life and the best person to decide what is in my best interests is me.

I don't need to prove anything to anyone any more, I am a smart articulate young lady (Derek winked as he recognised his own words) but even if I wasn't – I could have been asked, me and lots of other people like me.

I am disabled, I can't think quickly like you, but I have de, deter, deter..."

"Determination" Diane mouthed.

"Determination – I know what I want and with some help I can usually achieve it. Thank you."

The room was silent. Everyone stared at her, not knowing how to react. Diane started to clap, rapidly followed by the whole room. Within seconds everyone was standing up and clapping loudly. Jess beamed with pride as Derek clapped his heads above his head. She could see tears in Diane's eyes as the presenter, now put in his place, shook her hand as an equal.

"Well, Jess, you've given us a lot to think about."

"I hope so," Jess smiled, returning to her seat.

The service user/carer relationship between Diane and Jess slowly dissolved over the following ten years. After Alan's sudden death in 2001, Diane was conscious that she was increasingly reliant on Jess to help out and this worried her.

Sandra's health deteriorated at this time, and Jess seemed to instinctively step into Alan's shoes in terms of helping with her care.

Diane wasn't alone in her concerns, eventually Sandra's Care Manager, Graham, suggested that it was not fair on either of the girls to continue the way things were.

"Sandra deserves to have her needs met appropriately and I think you should consider somewhere that can provide this."

In 2008, Diane, now in her seventies, and with very little fight left in her, reluctantly agreed.

The place Graham had earmarked was, in everyone's opinion, more suitable for Sandra. It was a new bungalow, one of three on a corner plot. All of them were adapted with wide doors, hoists, profiling beds and en-suite bathrooms.

Diane and Jess visited every Tuesday without fail. They took turns to push Sandra's wheelchair down to the shops and up the steep slope back.

Building work continued around the bungalow as more and more beds were requested.

"Business is doing well," the manager, Damien, confided in Diane. "We've just bought the plot next door and we're planning to build a lovely new centre for people with learning disabilities. We should get around thirty people in there, shops and leisure facilities too."

"Wow!" Diane reflected.

"They had shops at Oakwood!" Jess cut in.

"Well, yes, but this isn't Oakwood, it's a state of the art new build, a real community."

"Oakwood was a community, they said it had to close because it wasn't right to have so many people with disabilities living together."

"Well, whatever they said -" Damien gestured speech marks around the word 'they', rolling his eyes towards Diane and adding "we've got big plans and six or seven names down already."

"Can we go and look at it please?" Diane asked politely.

"Yes, of course." Damien seemed to be slipping into salesman mode. "Do you want me to show you around?"

"No" Diane snapped, her head already hurting with the sound of his voice.

Outside, the sun shone on the new site. Two builders were sitting outside a pre-fabricated cabin eating sandwiches and basking in the August heat.

"We're going to come full circle" Diane whispered, surveying the huge site in front of her.

Jess smiled, not really sure what she meant.

"Do you think we'll ever get it right, Jess?"

"Probably not" Jess giggled, pushing her arm through Diane's. Catching each other's eyes, they laughed, loudly, as they turned and walked back to the car.

Lightning Source UK Ltd.
Milton Keynes UK
UKOW050602240212

187876UK00001B/1/P